Dedication

This book is dedicated to Paul, Sandie, Wendy and Katy – my beloved children – without whom my life would be a much poorer place.

Christina Cornwell

ON THE ROAD TO RUIN

AUSTIN MACAULEY PUBLISHERS™

LONDON · CAMBRIDGE · NEW YORK · SHARJAH

A CIP catalogue record for this title is available from the British Library.

ISBN 9781788230872 (Paperback)
ISBN 9781788230889 (E-Book)

www.austinmacauley.com

First Published (2018)
Austin Macauley Publishers Ltd.
25 Canada Square
Canary Wharf
London
E14 5LQ

Acknowledgements

Many thanks to Arthur and Ada Cornwell, my parents. They gave me a wonderful education and so much love, even when I was a little` toad.

Chapter 1

It was the 30th of May, 1961. A typical late spring day. The sun was shining and the birds were all chirping in the churchyard. The cherry trees at the edge of the graveyard were in full bloom. A few pink petals were caught up in the breeze and blew from the churchyard onto the adjacent platform of the railway station.

A perfect day, but not for everyone.

The boy and girl stood on the platform, waiting for the London bound train. No words were spoken. Occasionally they glanced across the tracks at the large red brick railway house, the boy's parental home.

A net curtain twitched, but no face was apparent.

The hoot of the approaching train was heard, and with a screech of brakes and a flurry of steam, the great iron engine came to a halt.

A moment's hesitation and the large blue suitcase was heaved up into the carriage by the boy.

The girl stood for a moment still hoping that something would happen to stop this thing happening.

Reluctantly she stepped up into the compartment and numbly sat next to the boy.

The journey to London and the transit over to Euston became a blur.

Once on the northbound train, it all started to become reality.

Clackity clack, clackity clack. The train thundered on into the unknown.

A heaviness seemed to be rooting itself into the girl's stomach and the boy…no one could know what was going on in his head.

At Doncaster, the train stopped. People alighted and more got on.

The girl glanced at her companion, tears were coursing down his face.

They clung together, their tears mingling.

There were no words, it had all been said!

It was as though they were on a runaway train, nothing could stop what was round the corner, and neither knew what was waiting there.

They pulled apart and knew that to touch once more would be a mistake.

The train pulled into Leeds station, a glass domed cavern!

Terrifying. People rushing everywhere and the noise was deafening.

She knew he had to leave her, he knew he had no option.

The southbound train for his return was already waiting on another platform. They climbed the steps, he carried the case. At the top, he put the case down. He turned and touched her arm, couldn't bear to look into her eyes and ran to the steps down to his waiting train.

She stood watching as the southbound train left the station, till it disappeared round the bend into the mist.

A lump in her throat, a tear stained face, the total fear of the unknown.

Abandoned, just her and the big blue case.

She went and stood by the ticket office. The arrangement was that someone would come to the station to meet her. After 15 minutes she went outside the station and approached the first taxi in the queue waiting outside. She showcd the driver the address of her destination and he loaded the case into his cab.

The blue case!

Her mother had thrown all her daughters belongings into the case with great venom. If she could have thrown her daughter in, she would have done so, such was her anger.

Poor mother! What a terrible daughter she had been.

"After all we have done for you. It's the road to ruin!"

Her mother's words rang in her ears, probably would for many years.

On the journey, all Annie could see through the fog were tall factory chimneys and a lot of bustling traffic.

The taxi seemed to be travelling for over half an hour. Eventually, the taxi turned into a driveway through high stone walls.

A large Georgian style house appeared through the gloom.

Annie shuddered and the fear in the pit of her stomach became an actual pain.

A person came down the steps and peered into the taxi asking Annie's name.

The driver turned to her and asked her if she was sure she wanted to be here.

Annie often wondered in the following months what would have happened if she had asked the taxi driver to take her away. He obviously knew the house and its reputation.

The woman tapped on the window and told Annie to hurry and get out of the taxi. The woman paid the driver after he had deposited her case on the driveway.

The woman marched back up the steps into the house leaving Annie to struggle up the steps behind her.

"Follow me and hurry we haven't got all night. You are too late for tea. I will show you your room. After you have emptied your case, leave it outside the room and come back down the stairs to the kitchen, I will find you something to eat."

She showed Annie a battered chest of drawers where she was to put her clothes. As she unpacked her case, the woman searched her possessions before allowing Annie to place her things into the drawers. Her pockets were also searched much to Annie's consternation.

The room had five iron-frame beds, with one pillow to each bed, and each with a very washed out and threadbare woven cover.

The walls were painted a sickly pale green and the paint was peeling in places.

Annie had never seen such a dilapidated room.

She put her case outside the room and made her way back down the uncarpeted stairs where she found the large kitchen.

A plate with two pieces of dried up toast were thrust at her with a packet of Echo margarine, and a jar of jam.

Annie was almost too tired to eat, but somehow managed to swallow the toast.

When she had finished eating, the woman led her from the kitchen through the entrance hallway to a passage leading to a large sitting room. There were several girls in this room, some nodded at Annie, some carried on reading others seemed totally absorbed in their own thoughts.

This was the start of the journey, to what or where Annie had no idea.

Annie just sat in a corner. She had never felt so alone.

The nights were the worst. Annie's bed was under the dormer window.

Many nights she sat on the window ledge just watching the mist engulf the chimney pots, too tired to sleep and too tired to try and make sense of her situation. It was a place away from the horror of the day and the nightmares that sleep would bring.

Tears and yet more tears until there were no tears left, the feeling of absolute loneliness and abandonment.

Often she heard the sobs of the other girls. Their tossing and turning, and mumbled words as sleep was being invaded by the things going round in their heads not allowing them to rest.

Her mother's words still rang in her ears. The bruises on her back were fading, but the memory was still there of the wooden coat hanger that her mother had beaten her with.

Her mother so afraid of what the neighbours would say about her daughter on whom she had pinned such great hopes. But no, her daughter was a disgrace to the family.

She was now an outcast, a miscreant, no longer worthy to be in society.

"On the road to ruin."

Her parents in conjunction with her boyfriend's parents had found a place as far away from home as possible, to remove the 'problem' as it was referred to.

Hence the long journey into oblivion. A nursing course was the excuse used to explain her absence. Problem removed – return home as if nothing had happened.

"What planet did these people live on?"

Chapter 2

The house was to all outward appearances a private nursing home. The private patients came when they went into labour and had excellent one to one attention. No more than four to six private patients came at one time at a large cost.

The private suite was plush and decorated to a high standard.

The nursing staff highly qualified and smart in their starched uniforms.

Sister Green, Sister Croft both midwives and two trained nurses presided in the delivery and after care wards.

The wide carpeted stairs to this suite were totally out of bounds to the pregnant girls. The front entrance was also a no-go area during evening visiting hours.

The 'fallen' girls, as they were often described, arrived at the house at varying stages of their pregnancies. Mostly a couple of months prior to their due date, but some as Anna were sent to the house before the pregnancy became obvious. The maternity benefit books handed over to the management on arrival.

All the girls had their duties. The stone floors were scrubbed daily. The food preparation, cooking and cleaning duties were all done by the girls starting at six a.m. each morning.

The hardest job was across the rear yard in the laundry. All the soiled bed linen and terry nappies had to be boiled and scrubbed daily. There were no washing machines just large galvanized sinks where the soiled linen was soaked overnight.

They were then removed first thing in the morning scrubbed by hand before being immersed into galvanized electric boilers.

They had to be prodded and agitated by dollies until the stains disappeared.

The sinks were then filled with fresh cold water and the items taken from the boilers and rinsed three times in the three sinks, after which they had to be put through the wooden rollers of the antiquated mangles to remove as much water as possible. The linen was then hung on the multitude of washing lines that festooned the yard.

A member of the staff would inspect the sheets and nappies and frequently they would be ripped off the washing lines and thrown back at the girls to do again.

Annie was given this job and found it very hard. Every day there were dozens of nappies, sheets and pillowcases, it seemed never ending. Annie's hands became very sore and chapped with the cold water and detergents, and at the end of the day her fingers bled after she had finished her laundry duties.

The girls worked from six in the morning only stopping for a half hour lunch break where sandwiches were offered and a cup of tea. At four o'clock, as long as the chores were completed the girls were allowed go to the sitting room where they were supposed to knit or sew. They also wrote their letters at this time, which had to be submitted to the superintendent for her to read.

Any detrimental remarks in their letters were blackened out or the letter destroyed by the staff, incoming mail was also read before being given to the girls.

Annie's fingers were too sore for the first few weeks to sew or knit. Florence Sampson, the staff member who supervised the recreation time in the afternoons, gave Annie some Vaseline for her fingers. This had been the first kindness shown to her.

Annie was told by her roommates that the work would continue till their babies were born, then as soon as they were able, usually the day after giving birth for the following six weeks. During this six weeks the arrangements were made regarding their babies' futures.

In this final six weeks, the girls were allowed an afternoon out to visit the town. They were given two shillings and six pence to purchase toiletries and their bus fare.

Most nights the girls were too tired for long conversations. They were told not to discuss their personal situations with each other, but slowly as the girls got to know each other their stories were shared.

Chapter 3

There were four girls who shared Annie's room.

Margot had the next bed, she came from York. She was 19 years old, not a pretty girl, tall and lanky, but Annie soon learned that Margot although outwardly loud and brash, actually had a heart of gold.

She had often in the first few weeks comforted Annie as she sat and wept.

Margot told Annie how she had come to be in the house, it was a sad tale.

Margot had worked in a grocery store near to her home. She had worked there from the time she had left school.

She enjoyed the work. Her father had been a miner but had given up working underground as he had contracted lung disease. Her mother went 'skivvying' as Margot put it and Margot had left school to help to keep the roof over their heads.

Margot's employer had a son, who did the deliveries for his father and also worked in the shop.

Margot was flattered by the attention the son had given her, and she mistakenly thought that the son felt the same way as she did about him. One thing led to another and the cuddles and kisses in the stock room ended up in a quick coupling one evening when the son had been left by his father to close up the shop.

Margot realized a couple of months later that she was pregnant.

Her parents were horrified and marched straight down to her place of employment to confront her employer and his son.

It all turned nasty, with her boss accusing Margot of lying that his son was the father.

Margot's father grabbed the son by the scruff of his neck and the son quickly admitted that he had had sex with Margot, but said that she had wanted it and had led him on. Then he said some really nasty things about Margot.

Poor Margot was so hurt, as she thought that he had loved her. Too discover her beau's true feelings about her had left her traumatized.

Margot told Annie all this one day in the laundry when Annie found her weeping into a sink of stinking nappies.

Margot's parents were in their late fifties and neither financially or physically could they cope with another mouth to feed. So the decision had been taken by Margot and her parents that an adoption would be the best option for everyone.

Margot also felt that she did not want a constant reminder of her stupidity and she would felt she would not be able to love a child in these circumstances.

Annie and Margot forged a friendship. Although Margot's baby was due soon after Annie's arrival, she was still expected to work in the laundry. Annie helped her as much as she could. After they had finished their work they started to sit together in the rest room.

The girls were supposed to bring clothes for their babies to wear for the first six weeks and Margot had brought some hand-me downs that her mother had managed to gather from neighbours. Annie had washed these baby clothes for Margot and they had come up quite presentable.

Three weeks after Annie's arrival, Margot went into labour. Annie was anxious about her friend. She had no idea what labour pains were like and was horrified at the intensity of the pain her friend was experiencing.

Margot was hustled up to the labour ward, which was in a small wing round the corner from the private wards, at the back of the house.

No news came about Margot by bedtime and Annie couldn't sleep for worrying about her friend.

The next morning after breakfast as Annie was sluicing the filthy nappies in the laundry, Miss Sampson, who had given Annie the Vaseline for her sore fingers, came over and quietly told Annie that her friend was OK and she had given birth to a little boy.

The following day Margot returned to work and her son was put into the nursery set aside for the girl's babies.

The mothers had to feed, bath and dress their infants at six in the morning before having their own breakfasts. Then work till ten o'clock, and again go and feed their child. It was a strict regime, six o'clock, ten o'clock, two, six and finally ten at night. In between these feeds, the work still had to be completed.

Annie now understood why the girls who had given birth were always so exhausted.

Margot was sent back to the laundry to do the ironing as this was lighter than the washing, so at least she could have a chat with Annie.

Margot seemed besotted with her little son, which surprised Annie.

She had called him Sonny Jim, and related his cute looks, and his tufty hair and mannerisms to Annie repeatedly.

This worried Annie as she knew that Margot was going to have to say goodbye to the little chap and felt she was getting too attached to him.

Annie tried to talk of other things to try and divert Margot from Sonny.

One of the girls in the house looked very young and Annie asked Margot about her, in attempt to get Margot's attention elsewhere.

"Oh that is Norma, she is only 14 years old. She was in the care of the social services, and has been in foster homes since she was three years old."

Norma would not talk to the other girls, but she did occasionally speak to Margot. Her bedroom was across the hall from Annie and Margot's, sharing with two older girls, to whom she rarely communicated.

"What a sad life, I wonder how she got pregnant? Perhaps she was attacked."

"She won't talk about it, I don't really think she understands what is happening to her. I know she cannot read or write very well. I do keep trying to get her to talk to me."

Annie did try a few times after her conversation with Margot to talk to Norma, but didn't get very much more than a yes or no or a shrug of her shoulders. But both girls kept trying as both had soft hearts and felt so sorry for the little girl.

Her worried little face and bitten fingernails showed that the strain of living in the house was having a bad effect on the girl. She no more than a child.

Margot got very tired and the laundry work was hard. Annie went round the back of the laundry building and found an old chair that had been discarded from the house, for Margot to sit on while she did the ironing. If a staff member came into the laundry, Margot would push the chair in a corner and throw a sheet over it, as the chair would have been confiscated straight away.

A week after Margot had returned to work, the two girls were wearily climbing up the stairs to their room to go to bed. Norma was following behind them. Suddenly Norma screamed and seemed to fall back down a couple of stairs clutching her stomach.

Margot and Annie went back down to Norma and realised there was fluid running down the stairs and blood on Norma's legs.

"Stay with her," shouted Margot. "I will go and get someone."

Annie took Norma's hand and put her other arm round her shoulders.

Within minutes, the nursing staff arrived, Margot and Annie were told to go to bed. The girls carried on up to their room, feeling sorry to leave little Norma.

A little later they heard the siren of an ambulance and realized it had come to the house.

Sleep didn't come easily to either of the girls that night.

The next morning when they enquired about Norma, they were told that Norma had been taken to hospital and her baby had been born dead. All the girls felt sorry for the young girl.

It seemed to leave a feeling of gloom on all the inmates, suddenly life and death had been introduced into the equation.

Margot asked the staff if she could go and visit Norma on her afternoon visit to town. She was sternly told that this was not possible or allowed and the girls were told not to speak of Norma again.

Later that day after Margot had returned from feeding Sonny, she told Annie that there was an extra baby in the nursery that morning.

"I asked old misery guts Clampton, the nursery nurse, whose baby it was and she told me to mind my own business. Then she said that it was belonging to one of the private patients who had a bad labour and needed extra rest!"

"So what was strange then?" Annie asked.

"Well it's still there and it's visiting time and surely the private patient would want to have their baby on show for visiting time."

"Mmm, does seem odd, but perhaps the mother is really poorly."

"He is obviously of mixed race, he is really cute. Oh well I suppose the private patients will have nannies to look after their babes so perhaps they don't get too possessive over them."

The conversation had to quickly cease as Mary Little, the laundry and kitchen supervisor was seen coming across the yard to the laundry building.

The discussion regarding the extra baby was not pursued again that day as both girls were so tired by the time they got to the recreation room. Annie tried to write a letter to her parents and Margot actually closed her eyes and had a nap.

That evening when they got to their beds it seemed that it was not a conversation that either of them wanted to discuss in front of their roommates, so the matter dropped.

The other three girls in their room were Doreen, Sharon and Marion.

Doreen was 18 years old and lived locally. She was a plump faced, heavily built, fair-haired girl with a pretty face and a friendly personality.

She had become pregnant by her boyfriend who she had been to school with, and their families were friends. But it had been decided, mainly by their respective parents that they were too young to start a family.

In 1961, girls were more respectful of their parents and unmarried pregnancies meant a shotgun wedding or a trip to a house such as this one the girls were in. So Doreen had agreed to do what her parents had thought best for her.

Marion was the eldest of the girls, she was 22. A tall thin faced girl with long light brown hair. All the girls knew that she had got pregnant by a married man and that he was a Jamaican. She had come to the house without her family's knowledge and made no secret of the fact that she wanted the child adopted, so that she could move on with her career. The married man had disappeared when she told him that she was pregnant, leaving Marion very anti-man.

Marion came across as a cold fish, but the girls heard her quiet tears as they lay in their beds all immersed in their own fears. They all knew Marion was hiding her grief, but they respected her need to cope with it in her own way.

Sharon was 17 and the noisy one. She obviously came from a wealthy family and boasted about her possessions and lifestyle. Her father was a wealthy businessman owning several companies. He had, according to Sharon, paid a large donation to the proprietors of the house for her to come to there at an early stage of her pregnancy. Her parents did not want their friends to be aware of the pregnancy.

Sharon made no secret of the fact that she had no idea which one of her many admirers was the father of her child, and didn't care either. She openly verbally abused the growing child inside her, and couldn't wait to get 'rid of the brat' as she called it!

It had been a big shock to her when a scrubbing brush and bucket had been given to her, and told to scrub the kitchen floor.

There had been a standoff with the staff when she point blank refused.

But her father had been summoned and he proved unsympathetic and threatened to wash his hands of her, and sell her horse if she didn't obey the rules of the house.

When she first arrived, she would leave her clothes and shoes laying all over the floor. The other girls just picked them up and threw them onto her bed in a heap. Slowly Sharon got better. She liked to be the centre of attention and would occasionally pick on Margot who was not as bright as her intellectually. The other girls wouldn't stand for this and made it clear that this was not acceptable as they all liked Margot.

The two older girls who had shared the bedroom with Norma, were Jane and Molly. They had both had their babies and were waiting with dread for the six week period to pass while the adoption processes were being negotiated.

Jane had become pregnant with a salesman who visited the office where she worked. They had begun a relationship and Jane was besotted by her boyfriend. When she told him that she was pregnant, he had persuaded her that he wasn't ready for a family so adoption had been decided upon.

Molly had never discussed the father of her baby and Jane had respected the fact that Molly didn't want to talk about it.

Chapter 4

Margot now having had her child was allowed one afternoon out of the house to go to town. It was a bit of freedom always looked forward to by the girls. So two weeks after Sonny was born Margot went to town. She knew the permitted time was short, only three quarters of an hour to shop and then back on the bus. If a girl missed the bus back to the house, then they would be sent to their room with no food that evening and the following week's trip was cancelled.

With Margot away for the afternoon it meant that Annie had to complete the washing and the ironing by herself and consequently did not get back to the day room until just before supper was served.

At the supper table, Margot whispered to Annie that she had something to tell her, but would tell her later away from staff ears.

But that night Annie was exhausted. After a quick wash in the antiquated washroom, she climbed into bed and as soon as her head hit the pillow she fell asleep.

The next morning after a breakfast of the hateful bowl of salty porridge that Yorkshire people seemed to delight in, the girls went over to the laundry to start the days washing and ironing.

The smell from the soaking soiled terry nappies always made Annie want to retch and this morning was no different. It was at this point of the day when the girls were at their lowest. They had washboards to scrub the faeces from the nappies before they were put into the boilers. The soiled sheets from the delivery room also had to be scrubbed before going into the boilers.

Conversations at this point were rare as the girls tied pieces of old sheets around their faces to combat the smell.

While the boilers were getting hot the girls went into the ironing room at the rear of the laundry. Margot made a small rolled up cigarette with the tobacco she had bought on her day off, and lifted the sash window so the smoke would escape.

"I have been dying to tell you, I saw Norma in town yesterday. They have allowed her to escape this place. Think the Welfare had something to do with it. She was with her new foster mother they have found for her."

"Oh poor Norma, did she speak to you?"

"Yes, this new foster mother looked really nice. Norma said that she was actually a distant cousin of her real mother. Norma said she was very nice and had found a school near her house and they had just been to see it. Norma is actually looking forward to starting when she is well enough."

"That sounds great. Did she say anything about her baby?" Annie asked.

"Well that was strange. She told me that after the nurses took her up to the delivery room, she had a few pains and then the baby was born."

"So it was born dead?"

"That was what we were told but Norma said the baby cried 'like a good un,' as she put it."

Annie looked puzzled, "But the baby couldn't have been born dead if it cried."

"That's what I thought, but I didn't say much more as Norma seemed upset that it had died so I said nothing."

"And there is the 'extra baby' in the nursery the morning after Norma was taken to hospital."

They heard footsteps coming across the yard so Margot quickly closed the window and hurried back to the now bubbling boilers.

Both girls were thoughtful all day, something didn't seem right.

Chapter 5

All the girls had to work very hard. Jane and Molly who had already had their babies, worked on the private wing, cleaning and waiting on the private patients. They were not allowed to hold conversations with the patients apart from 'good morning' or 'good evening'. They also prepared the private patients meals, which were considerably more nourishing than the food given to the girls.

Into the second week after Sonny Jim was born, Margot was moved to the private wards to work. She was sorry to leave Annie but to argue would have been useless. She was started on the cleaning duties and although she missed Annie the work was easier.

After she had fed Sonny, she would collect all the soiled linen from the wards and take them over to the laundry for Annie to put into soak. She then returned to have her breakfast with the other girls. This being the only time Margot saw Annie but conversation was limited as staff were often in and out of the laundry.

Margot got to know Jane and Molly as they all had to work together in the kitchen preparing the meals after the laundry and cleaning was done.

Jane had given birth to a little boy two weeks before Margot and Molly's little girl a few days earlier.

When they were feeding their babies, they were able to talk when the nursery nurse was not there. Jane was having second thoughts about the adoption and was hoping to persuade her boyfriend to agree to her keeping their son.

Molly told them that she had no option over keep Dinah, her baby. Her mother had a very serious heart condition and if she found out that Molly had been pregnant it would likely kill her. So she had told her mother that she had been given the chance of a four-month course in the London branch of her office. Her mother keen to enhance her daughter's career had insisted that she took the course, as Molly guessed she would. Arrangements had been made for her mother's sister to come and stay for the four months. Fortunately Molly was able to conceal her pregnancy from her mother and had come to the house when she was just over six months pregnant.

The two girls had become good friends, Jane confiding in Molly and Molly was a good listener, but rarely talked about her past or the dread of losing Dinah. But they both knew the adoptions were looming.

They had experienced several of the adoption days with other girls. Cruelly the mothers were given the new clothes that the adoptive parents had supplied to the home. The mothers had to bath and dress their babies in the new clothes and then say goodbye. They were then sent up to their bedroom to pack their own belongings.

All the girls were aware of the adoption days; a gloom fell onto the house. It was the 'sword of Damocles' hanging over all the girls' heads. They knew their turn would come soon for the final goodbye.

The bedroom that Jane and Molly shared was in the front of the old house. The bedroom window was above the front door, so on adoption days the girls would creep up the stairs and watch for the adoptive parents to arrive.

The mother of the child was usually beside herself with grief by the time the car arrived. But the girls did their best to console her.

The cars were always top of the market vehicles. This did give some comfort to the mothers to know that the new parents would be able to give their child much more than they could.

The final sight of the woman holding their beloved baby and then driving away was a devastating experience for the baby's mother and the other girls as well.

Jane and Molly had seen too many of these days. It was heart breaking.

The distraught girl was then told to leave the house, leaving their hearts in pieces. Memories that would never leave them.

At supper on adoption days, the empty chair and in the nursery the empty cot, a stark reminder of what was to come to them all!

Chapter 6

The work situation continued, Annie stayed in the laundry. Her hands had got hardened to the scrubbing and detergents. Doreen, who shared her bedroom now replaced Margot.

The extra baby was still in the nursery. The nursery nurse fed and changed him before the girls arrived to see to their babies.

Margot told Annie that all the private patients all seemed to have their babies beside them in the ward and as far as Margot could see all the mothers appeared to be white.

"Perhaps it is the father who is coloured," Annie said. "And perhaps one of the mothers had twins."

Margot went to the dustbins behind the laundry every day to deposit the vegetable peelings and kitchen waste. Annie would look out for her and would slip out between the billowing sheets on the washing lines so that the staff in the house would not see her going to talk to Margot.

" Tonight I am going to leave it as late as I can to collect the dirty dinner plates, then I might see the fathers arrive and see if any of them could be the little man's daddy."

"I was talking to the little one this morning after I had fed Sonny and Old Clampton gave me a right telling off."

"Yes I got a telling off too yesterday as I went through the front hall when there was a visitor in the office," Annie said.

The staff were always creeping about so their afternoon conversations had to be brief.

Jane found Molly in tears in their bedroom the next day.

"Dinah has got a heart defect," she told Jane.

"They cannot place her for adoption until the problem is properly investigated, so I cannot leave till it's done."

Molly was worried, as her aunt was due to return home soon and this would mean her mother would be on her own.

The adoption had been scheduled for ten days' time and Molly's return home planned.

Poor Molly was devastated at the thought of parting with her daughter, but knew she had no choice and now the worry of her mother only added to her problems.

The next day, Jane went to town to meet her boyfriend, her son's father.

Molly had smuggled her camera into the house on her arrival, as she intended to at least have a photo of her child. She had managed to take a couple of snaps of Jane's son also when Mavis Clampton, the nursery nurse had gone over to the kitchen. On their half day trips to town, the girls had managed to get the film developed and Jane had been delighted to have a photo of Jonathon, her son to show her boyfriend.

Annie often took a quick stroll in the large garden before she went over to the main house after she had finished in the laundry. The garden had lots of tall shrubs so it was easy to stay out of sight of the staff so she could have a few minutes of solitude.

On the day of Jane's visit to town, Annie found Molly sitting on the grass behind the huge pampas grasses in tears.

Annie sat down beside her and Molly told Annie about her fears for her daughter and about the worry of her mother being left on her own.

There was nothing Annie could say, but she was a good listener and it helped Molly to unload her problems.

When Jane returned from town, she was jubilant. On seeing the photos of his son, her boyfriend had agreed that they should keep their son. His widowed mother had recently got remarried and her house was to be given to her son. Jane's boyfriend had asked her to marry him and they would move into his mother's house. It all seemed perfect.

Molly was so pleased for her friend that it took her mind away from her own troubles for a short time.

On informing the superintendent of the change of plan, she was told that she would still have to stay for the agreed six weeks before she could leave the house. The staff were not happy, as now the planned adoption would be cancelled, 'at great inconvenience' as Jane was told. But it only meant a delay of a couple of weeks and the wedding had to be planned.

Jane asked if Molly could be allowed to attend the registry office for her wedding as her bridesmaid. After several arguments and pleading this was granted.

The wedding gave the girls something pleasant to talk about, not that any of them apart from Molly were going to be allowed to attend.

The situation with Dinah did not seem to be getting solved quickly. The doctors still could not give her a clean bill of health so her adoption was on hold.

Chapter 7

At breakfast time the day after Jane's good news, Margot whispered to Annie that 'the extra baby' as they called him was not now in the nursery, but had been moved up to the private wing to a small side room.

She had left picking up the dirty supper dishes as late as she dared and had seen all the visitors as they had come up the stairs. All the visitors had been white, and she was sure that none of them visited the little room where the other baby was.

The next day Margot had her afternoon visit to town. She went to the market where Norma had told her that her foster mother had a stall. Norma was sitting by the stall and was pleased to see Margot. Linda, her foster mother told the girls to go to the café and have a cup of tea and a chat.

Norma asked how the other girls were and if the conditions in the house were still as bad.

"Two more babies have gone for adoption since you left. Alice's and Brenda's. They were in bits, Alice's mother came and picked her up and nearly had to carry her to her car, she was that upset. Brenda said nothing to any of us, but I could see she was choked."

"I would have liked to have at least seen my baby," Norma said wistfully.

"I remember you said that you heard your baby cry, but we were told it was born dead?" Margot poured out more tea into their cups and wondered if she should ask anymore.

"Yes he did cry, but they rushed him out of the room and later Sister Green came back in and said that unfortunately he had died, and then the ambulance came as I was losing a lot of blood and I had to go to hospital, but I never saw him."

Margot could see tears welling up in Norma's eyes, so she took her hand and said no more.

The girls finished their tea and went back to the market said their goodbyes and Margot had to run to catch her bus.

The next day at the dustbins Margot told Annie of the conversation. They both felt sad for Norma.

"She is so young, and has had some tough breaks in her life. She just wishes she had at least seen her little boy. At least, they did tell her that. She is a little rough diamond but underneath she is a nice kid."

"Stop that gossiping, you two." One of the staff had come across the yard.

"Just getting the washing in, Miss. It looks like rain," Annie said as Margot scuttled back to the kitchen.

Bitch, thought Annie.

Chapter 8

A few days later Doreen went into labour and the girls heard the following day that she had given birth to a little girl. As Doreen lived locally, her parents were able to visit. Visiting day was for an hour on a Saturday afternoon. As most of the girls came from other areas and some had not told their relatives where they were, there were very few visitors which pleased the staff.

On the Saturday following the birth of her daughter, her parents arrived at the house. They were allowed an hour to speak with their daughter but a member of staff was present throughout the visit.

Doreen's mother asked to see her granddaughter, but was told that this was not possible. Her father could not understand why they couldn't see the baby.

"As the child is to be adopted, we do not encourage families bonding with the child. This only makes the decision harder for everyone," was the explanation given.

Doreen got very upset and said "You have no idea what this place is like, Mum, we all work like slaves and the babies belong to them, we have no say."

The door opened and Agnes Dayton, the superintendent stormcd in.

"Now, Doreen, you know that is not true. We have looked after you and you have had the best medical care and we are only protecting the little one from infection. You do understand don't you?" she said turning to Doreen parents.

"Doreen's little girl is only days old and the sterile nursery is the safest place for her."

Doreen sat down deflated and her mother took her hand and said, "Perhaps Miss Dayton is right, love, we will come next week to see you."

After her parents were shown out of the house, Doreen was taken into the main office.

"I am very disappointed in your outburst Doreen. As a result, your visiting rights will be cancelled for the next two weeks. I will write to your parents to inform them. Now there are some forms I want you to fill in regarding the forthcoming adoption."

She pushed some documents across her desk to Doreen. Doreen stood up and pushed the papers onto the floor and ran out of the office and up to her room where she collapsed onto her bed sobbing.

Annie was in their bedroom having slipped up to fetch some tissues. She went and sat on Doreen's bed and took her hand.

"They are going to stop my mum and dad from visiting for two weeks and they wouldn't let them see Danielle. Then she wanted me to sign some papers. I am sure if my mum and dad saw her they would let me keep her. I won't sign those bloody papers, I won't." Doreen subsided into loud heart-rending sobs.

Annie thought for a moment. "How about I ask Molly if she will take some photos of Danielle so you can show your mum and dad? She did it for Jane. Can't promise she will, but I can ask her."

Doreen immediately stopped crying and agreed that Annie should try and persuade Molly to take the pictures.

Doreen dried her eyes and the two girls went down to the sitting room and settled to their books and sewing.

Some of the girls were knitting things for Jane's baby as wedding presents. Miss Sampson the staff member who supervised the craft and recreation time was embroidering a beautiful tablecloth for the happy couple. She told her colleagues that she was demonstrating embroidery techniques to the girls, as it would have been frowned upon by Miss Dayton if it was known she was doing something nice for one of the girls.

Miss Sampson was the only member of staff that the girls really liked. But she had to maintain a superior attitude in front of the other staff members.

Unlike her colleagues she never belittled any of the girls or made them feel like second-class citizens because they were unmarried mothers. She often shuddered when she heard some of the insults that were hurled at the girls at times.

Annie waited till she went up to bed that night and crossed the landing and tapped on Molly and Jane's door. Molly let her in and when Annie asked her if she would help Doreen, she agreed straight away. She said that it would be risky as Nurse Clampton watched them all like a hawk.

"One of us could cause a diversion, and she does have to go to the storeroom in the kitchen to get more milk powder when we are getting low," Annie said.

Molly thought for a moment. "The tin is getting low at the moment, we could try tomorrow. I will take my camera and hope she buzzes off for a minute or two."

Annie gave Molly a hug and quickly left the room only to bump into Brenda Jones the staff member who patrolled the corridors to check that the girls were all in their rooms.

"Why are you in the wrong room, lady?"

"Just returning a comb I borrowed from Molly," Annie replied and ran back to her own room. She gave the thumbs up to Doreen as she got into her bed.

Doreen was still upset that her parents were not allowed to visit for the following two weeks. However, her father rang Agnes Dayton and informed her that whatever she said they were going to visit on the second week as it was Doreen's mother's birthday, and she wanted to see her daughter that weekend.

Miss Dayton was no match for George Cooper and agreed that they could visit in two weeks' time.

Annie found a pack of cards and the next Saturday after she had finished in the laundry she started to teach Doreen and Margot to play some games. This helped to pass the time for Doreen who was a little happier when she had been told her parents would be visiting the following weekend.

The girls couldn't discuss the plan to take the photos of Danielle in the sitting room. Although Miss Sampson was nice, they couldn't take the risk that she may feel obligated to tell someone.

They had to wait until the Monday before the opportunity presented itself for Molly to get photos of Danielle. Mavis Clampton had to go to the storeroom as Molly had predicted to get more milk powder for the nursery.

Margot was going to town the following day and promised to take the film into the chemists to be developed. Jane was going to town on the Friday and was going to pick the photos up, so that Doreen could give them to her parents somehow on their visit.

After Margot had delivered the film to be developed, she wandered round the market to see Norma. Her aunt, as Norma had started to call Linda, was at her stall and greeted Margot with a smile.

"Hello, Margot, how are you?" she said in between serving customers.

"Ok thanks, where is Norma?"

"She has gone back to school and is really enjoying it. She was never given any encouragement to learn, but she has a special teacher who knows all about her background and is taking a lot of care of her. She left a note in case you called to see her."

Linda gave Margot a scrap of paper and on it were seven words.

'Thank you for being my friend. Norma x'

"She is picking up reading and writing so quickly, we are so proud of her."

Margot knew all the girls would be as pleased as her to hear that little Norma was getting on so well.

"You know we are very sorry we didn't find her sooner. We would have looked after her and her little one. It wouldn't have mattered that the child was of mixed race. Yes, Norma has opened up to us a bit about her life, but there is more to come we think. My husband and I were never lucky enough to have children of our own, but we both love Norma. My husband is a police sergeant and has seen some things but Norma's treatment as a child was awful, but now she is safe, we are thinking of asking if we can adopt her."

Margot left the market feeling very happy for her friend, but there was something that bothered her.

Chapter 9

All the girls were getting very tired. The late August weather was very humid. The private wing was very full so there were a lot of extra sheets and nappies for Annie to scrub. Her hands had hardened to the work but her increased size was making it harder each day.

The girls who worked in the house were complaining about the heat and the extra work.

Sharon still maintained she wanted to lose the bump and get back to her wonderful life. Her parents had not made contact with her since she had arrived. The other girls got fed up with listening to her boasting about her marvellously rich friends and lifestyle.

Her parents were 'well minted' as she put it. Daddy owned several large companies and Mummy was from a titled family and spent most of her time in spars (which Margot had thought she meant the grocery shops) and on the golf course.

It seemed that neither parent had given Sharon much of their time. She had been brought up by nannies and sent to boarding schools from which she had been expelled several times. She needed to be the centre of attention and as the other girls now ignored her she took delight in saying outrageous things to get their attention.

She was the next to go into labour. She started to complain of backache as the girls were getting into bed. By midnight, it was obvious it was time to get her over to the delivery ward.

The girls knew that no one would come to their room so the girls put on their dressing gowns and helped Sharon down the stairs and across the hallway to the stairs leading up to the wards. They got her to the bottom of the carpeted stairs and Sharon collapsed in a spasm of a contraction. Annie sprinted up the stairs to get some help.

She heard voiced coming from one of the outer rooms leading to the private wards.

"So he is going shortly, well that's a relief I am getting fed up with the feeding and changing him. I suppose the welfare have arranged it all, seems odd though."

Annie had hesitated when she heard the conversation, but a squeal from Sharon at the bottom of the stairs made her tap on the door and shout for some assistance.

"What you doing up here, girl, how long have you been at the door?"

"I have just come up the stairs please can you help, Sharon is in labour at the bottom of the stairs."

The two midwives went down the stairs and unceremoniously hauled the groaning Sharon up the stairs and told the rest of her roommates to go back to bed.

Sharon's language was getting worse with each contraction and the girls had to smile as they went back across the hall to go up their stairs.

Sharon screamed at the nurses, sentiments not usually heard from young ladies.

"Oh well at least we will have a peaceful night," Margot said as they all climbed back into their beds.

Chapter 10

The staff in the house were all women except old Tom, who came to cut the grass and tidy the garden twice a week. He was 70 years old, a retired council worker. He lived just up the road from the house, and was happy to get the job after he had retired. He kept himself to himself and had been instructed on taking the job that he was not to speak to any of the girls.

Occasionally he would slip into the laundry and have a natter with Annie and have his cup of tea from the flask he brought with him. He lived alone and enjoyed having someone to talk to. He seemed to have a second sense when any of the staff were approaching the laundry and made himself scarce very quickly.

Secretly he was unhappy at all the work that the girls were expected to do, but he kept his opinions to himself.

The superintendent, Agnes Dayton had been in charge of the house for the last five years. She was a fifty seven year old spinster and was totally engrossed in her job. She had been brought up by very strict parents, her father being an Anglican vicar and her mother a little mouse who obeyed her bully of a husband without question.

In Agnes's world, her word was law, her decisions were never to be questioned and she had no sympathy with the situation that the girls found themselves. She had never had a physical relationship with a man or a woman, and the only thing that excited her was money and the power over her subordinates.

She had always been a plain looking girl, a bit on the chubby side. Never used make up and always had her hair cut as short as possible. Her only friend, or the only person she tolerated was Alice Green, the senior midwife. They had both started at the house at the same time and it was thought by colleagues that they may have known each other before their appointment at the house.

Grace Maggs was technically the second in command. But this was a joke, as Grace knew that she had to do exactly as Agnes ordered, otherwise her life would be a complete misery. So Grace never contradicted Agnes.

She carried out most of the secretarial duties, answering the phone and when Agnes made an unpopular decision it always fell to Grace to be the one to deliver the news to the unfortunate recipient.

Grace was a tall thin woman of 62 years old, but she had lowered her age on her application form when she applied for the position as she thought this would enhance her chances of obtaining the post. She had dark hair which she was glad only had a few grey hairs and she kept it pulled back in a severe bun. She was actually a kind woman and often she despaired of the severe decisions that Agnes inflicted on the girls, but she kept her thoughts to herself.

Alice Green, the senior midwife dealt mainly with the girls' pregnancies. She had been married many years ago, but her spouse had got sick of her acid tongue and they had parted after a couple of years. She had a pale freckled face and frizzy ginger hair. Alice was approaching 50, but would never discuss her actual age.

One evening a week, she would spend a couple of hours in Agnes's sitting room for a game of chess, or that is what the staff were told. The evening chosen was usually the day after Alice had been out of the house on her day off, when she drove off in her Morris Minor car.

Florence Sampson, the craft teacher, and general 'dogs body' as she thought of herself, disliked Alice Green and

Agnes. So she kept her head down, and carried out her duties as quietly as possible.

Florence had looked after her aged parents until they had both passed away five years ago. She had been courted by a neighbour's son for several years but he had eventually got tired of waiting for Florence and had moved to London where he had met someone else and was now married with a family.

Florence sometimes wondered how different her life could have been, but she never regretted the time she had spent with her beloved parents.

After her parents died she saw an advertisement in the Yorkshire post for this position as craft teacher and general assistant for which she had applied and was offered the job four years ago. She was not particularly happy in the house but approaching fifty-five years old she knew that employment would not be easy to find. She had rented out her parents' home to build herself a little nest egg for when she retired, so it suited her to live in the house.

She often disagreed with decisions made by Agnes but was wise enough to say nothing.

Mavis Clampton, the unpopular nursery nurse and Mary Baines the woman in charge of the kitchen also lived in the house and shared a room along the corridor from the girls' rooms.

The other midwife Sister Croft spent some nights in the house when she was on duty, but as she lived only a few miles away spent her off duty days at her home with her husband. She was a good midwife and only worked in the private wards and had very little to do with the girls. Privately she shared Agnes's view that the girls deserved little sympathy.

Brenda Jones did not live in. She worked afternoons and evenings and as a state enrolled nurse sometimes assisted Sister Green and Sister Croft in the labour wards. If they were very busy, Brenda would begrudgingly work extra hours. She could be very spiteful to the girls and delighted in telling tales if she saw any of the girls doing something considered wrong.

A couple of part time auxiliary nurses helped out in busy times but had nothing to do with the girls.

Chapter 11

Sharon's baby was born after a fairly quick labour. Her little boy was born with a lot of dark hair. Sharon although pretending indifference to her child crept out of bed to look into the cot beside her bed, while Mavis Clampton who had assisted Sister Green was clearing the soiled bed linen.

The tiny baby gazed back at his mother and Sharon gently touched his downy head.

If there is a moment when even a stony heart can be reached, then for a second something hit Sharon.

She burst into tears, not really sure why, and got back into her bed.

I hate babies, she thought. *What is the matter with me?*

Mavis came back into the room and lifted the child from his cot and put him into Sharon's arms.

"You probably won't have milk yet, but it doesn't hurt to suckle him, nothing like his mother's milk for his first feed. We will put him on the bottle tomorrow when he goes down to the nursery." With that she left a bewildered Sharon holding her baby.

Doreen's parents arrived on the Saturday after the week's enforced absence. Her father was not going to be refused entrance and was ready for an argument when the front door was opened by Grace Maggs. But no comment was made and Mr and Mrs Cooper were shown into the visitor's room. Grace asked them if they would like a cup of tea, an unusual happening but as Agnes had gone out for the afternoon with

Alice Green, Grace felt able to be more hospitable than when Agnes was in the house.

She was sure Agnes had arranged to be out when the Cooper's came for the visit as she hated not getting her own way, after he had made it quite clear that they were going to visit Doreen that weekend whatever she said.

When Grace left the room to organize the tea, Doreen handed her mother a paperback book.

"Hide this in your bag, Mum, before Maggs comes back, please don't let her see it, and don't open it until you get home."

Joyce Cooper quickly stowed the book into her capacious handbag. '

Grace returned with tea and put some papers on the table alongside the tray.

"There are some papers for you to sign, Doreen, perhaps you will feel happier to do it while your parents are here."

Grace had been given strict instructions from Agnes that the papers should be signed that day.

Mr Cooper picked up the papers and glanced through them

"These are legal papers I understand, concerning the adoption. Perhaps it would be good to get it out of the way love," he said turning to Doreen.

"Please Dad can I have a few more days, it all seems so final." Doreen's eyes filled with tears.

Her mother wrapped her arms around her daughter.

"Please don't cry, love."

Grace got up from her chair and picked up the papers from the table.

"I will delay things for a few days to give you time to make your decision. I will tell Miss Dayton that the papers will be signed a week on Monday without fail, is that agreeable to you Mr and Mrs Cooper?"

Doreen's parents could see how upset she was and nodded in agreement.

Grace knew she would get a roasting from Agnes for agreeing to delay the signing of the papers, but she would worry about that later.

She returned the papers to Agnes's office then went back to show the Cooper's out.

They were going to ask again to see the baby but as Doreen was so upset they left without mentioning it, which was a relief to Grace as she had been firmly told not to allow this. Grace knew that Mavis would delight in letting Agnes know that Grace had disobeyed her instructions.

After her parents had left Doreen asked if she could go up to her room and get a tissue. Grace knew that a few more tears were going to be shed so she allowed Doreen to escape to her room to calm herself down before going back to the sitting room with the other girls.

Jane's wedding was to be on the following Wednesday at the Registry Office in Leeds. The girls were helping Jane with her headdress and Miss Sampson had contributed some silk flowers from her now abandoned 'bottom drawer'. When Doreen returned to the sitting room, the girls were busily sewing a cream net veil to the flowery headband that Molly had made for Jane. The wedding was proving an enjoyable diversion for all the girls.

On the way home, Joyce Cooper took the book that Doreen had given her out of her handbag.

"Doreen knows I like a good tale, perhaps that's why she gave this to me."

As Joyce opened the book, two envelopes fell onto her lap. Joyce opened the top one labelled 'Mum and Dad.' She put her hand to her mouth and gasped as she looked at the photographs of Danielle.

"Oh my God, George oh George!"

She then saw the letter included with the photos, and as she read tears coursed down her face.

George drew the car into the curb and stopped, then took the letter from his wife's shaking hands.

'Dear Mum and Da

I have taken these photos of Danielle for you to see. She is so beautiful. Her eyes are as blue as the cornflowers in Gran's garden.

Please Mum and Dad I cannot give her to someone else. She takes my finger in hers and looks up at me and I swear she smiles.

No one else will ever love her as much as I love her.

Please, please do not make me do this, I will die if I have to lose her.

They will have to beat me before I will sign the adoption papers.

Please Mum she is your granddaughter, I know you will love her. I will do anything you want but not give her up.

I love you both but I cannot do this, please understand.

Doreen and Danielle xx

Even George felt a lump in his throat.

"That child is the image of our Doreen as a baby, but adoption would give them both a better start, love!"

Joyce wiped her eyes, and George restarted the car.

"The other letter is for Danny, should we give it to him?"

"Well, we have no right not to give it to him, it's what Doreen wants. I suppose he has a right to at least see a photo of his child. It might make him realize the consequences of their irresponsibility," George replied.

Chapter 12

Two days after her baby's birth Sharon returned to her cleaning duties.

The other girls who share her bedroom were a bit surprised as Sharon was not the noisy girl who had previously lived with them.

She would go up to bed with none of her usual comments and get straight into bed.

Margot tried to draw her into conversation, to no avail. Sharon just replied quietly with a 'yes or no' or a very brief reply.

When she was in the nursery, the girls noticed how gentle she was with her son. She had named him Dominic.

"I don't think she will part with him as easily as she thought," Margot told Annie.

"I think she is planning something as I saw her writing a long letter in the day room," Annie replied.

All the letters that the girls wrote had to be given to the office for the staff to read prior to posting, to ensure that the girls said nothing detrimental about the house or their conditions. Also all incoming mail was opened by Agnes or Grace, and sometimes the girls would receive only part of their letters, some of which were obliterated by a black marker pen if deemed inappropriate information for the girls to receive. This happened especially when Agnes was in charge.

The next day as Annie was boiling up the washing she was surprised to see Sharon coming across to the laundry building.

"I want to go and post a letter. Margot told me that she has a smoke in the ironing room with the window open, so how does the window open?" Sharon asked, looking at the big sash window.

Annie undid the catch and lifted the window.

Sharon climbed out saying, "Shut it down and I will tap on the window when I have been to the post box. If anyone is here snooping about, lean the broom up against the window and I will wait until they have gone."

Annie was on tenterhooks and anxiously kept a watch across the yard in case any of the staff were lurking.

The post box was only a few yards along the road and Sharon was soon back tapping on the window. Just as Annie was about to go through to the back room to open the window, Mavis Clampton appeared in the doorway. Annie picked up the broom and started to sweep up a few bits of fluff and placed the broom against the window. Sharon dived into the shrubbery opposite.

Mavis deposited an armful of soiled sheets onto the laundry floor saying, "Another couple of sheets for you to do, we are getting low as we have had two private patients deliver this morning, so get on with it!"

With that Mavis stomped out of the laundry.

Annie watched her disappear into the main house and then went and opened the window for Sharon to climb back inside.

"Wow that was close. Thanks, Annie, see you later," Sharon said as she darted back across to the main house.

That night as the girls were getting into bed, Sharon looked over at Annie winked her eye and gave Annie a smile.

Annie assumed that the afternoon's escapade was just between them and got into her bed happy that Sharon seemed a little more at ease.

Chapter 13

Wednesday dawned a sunny late September day. Jane and Molly were going to leave around 11 for the wedding in Leeds. A taxi had been ordered by Grace Maggs, requested by Molly who had offered to pay for this as a wedding present for Jane.

Baby Jonathon had been dressed in a new outfit provided by his father and Jane's case had been packed the evening before. Molly had to be back at the house by four in the afternoon. Nurse Clampton had reluctantly agreed to give Molly's baby Dinah, her midday feed.

Margot had promised Molly that she would keep an eye on Dinah and make sure she was winded and changed properly.

All the girls gave Jane a hug before she left with Molly to get into the taxi.

Jane looked lovely in a cream dress and the veil and head dress that the girls had helped her make.

Jane was thrilled with the beautiful tablecloth that Florence had embroidered which had been hidden in her case.

After they had left, all the girls went back to their duties, hustled by Agnes.

Everyone felt lifted by the happy event.

Molly had taken her camera to record the wedding so that she could show the girls on her return.

Annie was finding the laundry work very hard now as she was within a couple of weeks from her due date. She had a clinic visit at three that day and Nurse Croft was in charge of the clinic that day.

"Your blood pressure is a bit high Annie, I think it's time you were given lighter duties. I will notify Miss Dayton of this recommendation. Have you nearly finished today's laundry?"

"Only got to empty the boilers, Miss, and take the last of the nappies off the lines. They have dried well today."

"Go and do that then go and then put your legs up in the day room till suppertime. I will tell Miss Dayton."

Nurse Croft was certainly much nicer to the girls that Sister Green.

Molly returned just before four that afternoon and went straight into the nursery to make sure that little Dinah had been attended to. She then hurried back up to her room to get back into her working clothes.

As she changed, the pain she was feeling in her whole body exploded and she collapsed onto her bed. She covered her face with her pillow to muffle her sobs.

Annie, having finished in the laundry, went up the stairs to collect the book she was reading before she went to the day room.

As she passed Molly's room, she could hear a noise, not sure what she was hearing she tapped on Molly's door, and without waiting for a reply she crept in.

What she saw took her breath away.

Molly had her head under her pillow and she was punching the bedclothes obviously trying to disguise her distress.

Annie rushed over to her and put her arms round the quivering girl.

"Molly, what is the matter, please, Molly, talk to me?"

Molly pulled her head out from under her pillow. Her face was red and puffy and she was shaking.

"I can't tell anyone, it's so awful, so bloody awful."

Molly's voice shook and she sat on the side of her bed looking so forlorn.

Annie took her hand and put her other arm around her friend.

"Look, Molly, whatever it is I promise I will not to tell anyone, but something bad has obviously happened and you cannot keep all this hurt inside. A trouble shared they say can ease the load. Do you want me to get Florrie, she is always so kind? Perhaps you would prefer an older person?"

At that moment, Florence Sampson came into the room. She had come up to her room that was next door to Molly's to get a smaller size knitting needle. She had heard the tail end of Molly's noisy despair and had hesitated as to whether she should intervene.

When she had heard Annie mention her name as she hovered outside Molly's door, she made up her mind to investigate.

Chapter 14

A few miles away Joyce kept reading the letter from Doreen and looking at her granddaughter's photo. She had passed on the other letter to Danny and shown him the photos.

The lad had gone very quiet and had taken his letter to his home, where he read it in his room.

'My Darling Danny.

It is awful here and they are pushing me to sign the adoption forms.

I have asked my Mum to help me but not sure she will. I can't give our little girl up. I will run away with her if Mum won't help.

You said you would stick by me, just look at the photo of our lovely little girl, please don't let me down, I will die if they take her from me.

Next Monday morning can you get a car from your Dad's garage?

I will be waiting outside the house with Danielle, if you don't come I will get on the bus and take my baby where they can't find her or me.

We will try to be outside at 11 o'clock, please wait, but please come. I can't stand this place any longer.

I love you Danny

Doreen x

Danny didn't know what to do. He was terrified of George Cooper and had been lucky to escape a battering when they found out that Doreen was pregnant.

He lived with his widowed father next to the small garage his father owned a mile from Doreen's parents' home. His parents had been friends of long standing.

He adored Doreen and had many sleepless nights worrying about her being sent to the house and if the right decision was being made.

The picture of their little girl that Doreen had put in his letter had not left him since he received it. But he also saw the sense in waiting till they were older, what was he to do...?

Chapter 15

Florrie sat on the bed next to Molly.

"Whatever you tell me, Molly, it will go no further, and if there is anything I can do to help you, I will. Annie, you must make the same promise."

Molly wiped her eyes with the hanky that Florence had given her. She took a deep breath and not looking at either of them she falteringly began to talk.

"Jane looked so lovely and was so excited about getting married. When we got to the registry office, her mother was waiting outside. Her boyfriend, and his family were inside. We went in and her mother carried Jonathon and I followed behind. Jane turned round to give me her flowers. Then I saw her boyfriend!"

Molly burst into more tears and hid her face in her hands.

"It was him!" she sobbed.

"Who was it, Molly?" Florence gently asked.

"Dinah's father," Molly whispered.

Florence looked Annie and neither knew what to say!

"What did you do?"

"There was nothing I could do, I could not destroy Jane's chance of happiness, could I? So I said nothing. I had not told Dinah's father that I was pregnant. I had not made a connection that Jane's boyfriend James could be Dinah's father who I knew as Jim."

"What happened after the ceremony, James must have recognized you?"

Annie asked.

"When I was standing outside the registry office, he came over on the pretence of shaking my hand. He quietly asked me if I was going to tell Jane that we already knew each other or that we had an affair. All I could do was to shake my head," she said quietly.

"He must have been seeing me at the same time as Jane, as the two babies were only born two weeks apart."

Florence and Annie were shocked to the core. There were no words of consolation they could offer and nothing Florence could do to make things better for Molly.

Molly got up and rinsed her face in the hand basin in her room and brushed her hair.

"What will you do?" Florence asked.

"There is nothing I can do. Dinah will be adopted and I will go back to look after my mother and find a different job, so I won't bump into Jim again. I will keep in contact with Jane occasionally, but that will be all. Jane hadn't told anyone where we had met. She said that we were old school friends so that no one would know I have been here with her, so Jim need never know about Dinah. I just hope his philandering ways are over and he will be a good husband and father to baby Jonathon."

Florence was very impressed by Molly's magnanimous gesture but Annie felt very angry at the whole affair.

They all went downstairs to the day room where Molly gave the other girls a glowing account of the wedding. With all the upset she had forgotten to take any photos, so she told the girls that her camera had jammed and she hadn't been able to take any pictures. She said that Jane had promised to send her some so that kept the girls happy.

Molly much to the admiration of Florence and Annie just got on with her work and hid her heart break from everyone.

The heart problem that had been diagnosed in her baby was not giving too much concern and it had been decided that her adoption could go ahead.

Although Molly was aware that the adoption was imminent, the details of the adoptive parents were not divulged to her. She was told that the prospective parents had passed the assessment and the date for the parting was to be the following Monday.

Molly was dreading the day but tried to concentrate on the joy of being able to return home to her mother.

The adoptive parents who had been found were prepared to take Dinah, and were aware of the non-life threatening heart defect. In fact, the father was a cardiac surgeon and was not a bit fazed by her mild condition.

Florrie had seen the adoptive parents file when she had gone to collect Agnes's dirty supper plates. Agnes had left the file open and Florrie had taken a quick look while Agnes was outside her door giving one of the girls a dressing down about some trivial misdemeanour.

Florrie had quietly passed on the information about the occupation of the adoptive father to Molly. She knew Dinah's health issues were a concern for Molly.

All the girls were feeling a bit down when they knew that Molly's little girl would soon be gone, the euphoria of the wedding soon disappeared.

Molly's sad face told it all as she cuddled and fed her beautiful daughter.

"One more week, my darling," she whispered

But there was no other way and everyone knew this.

Chapter 16

The Saturday following the wedding, the Cooper's came to see Doreen again. The letters were not mentioned. Agnes was sitting in the room for the entire visit. She had not been at all pleased with Grace for allowing the signing of the adoption forms to be delayed. Agnes had made Grace's life a misery all week because of it.

Doreen was hoping that her parents would tell her that she could keep Danielle or at least say something, but nothing was said. Just idle conversation about her Gran's varicose veins and the antics of her cat.

As her parents were leaving, Agnes reminded Doreen that she had to come to her office on Monday to sign the paperwork for the adoption. But still nothing was said by her parents.

The following day Annie was now on kitchen duties with Doreen.

Marion had replaced Annie in the laundry along with a new arrival Rosalind.

Doreen was disappointed that Annie was no longer in the laundry but glad she was able to talk to her in the kitchen when Mary Baines the woman in charge of the kitchen was absent. Mary liked to sneak off into the garden and have a cigarette which suited the girls.

When Mary left for her mid-morning cigarette, Doreen grabbed Annie's hand and took her into the large pantry.

"Please, Annie, you have to help me. I was hoping you would still be working in the laundry so now I don't know what to do…"

Annie looked puzzled.

"I am going to take Danielle tomorrow and get away. I have asked Danny to get a car from his father's garage and come and collect me. I was going to climb out of the laundry window. Margot told me she used to have a ciggy in there with the window open. That window opens onto the back entrance and I could run down to the road from the laundry. But now you are not over there I am afraid that Marion might call the staff and I will be stopped."

"How are you going to get Danielle out of the nursery?" Annie asked.

"I don't know exactly but thought we could arrange a diversion to get rid of Clampton then I could get Danielle out."

Annie thought for a while then said, "We could use the milk powder again as we did to get the photos and I think Marion could be persuaded to help. But we would have to get rid of Rosalind as she is an unknown factor and may squeal to the staff."

At that moment, Mary returned smelling highly of cigarette smoke.

So conversation had to cease leaving Annie deep in thought.

Later that evening before climbing into bed Annie went across to Molly's room. Annie told Molly of the planned escape and Molly was eager to help and together they drew up a plan.

At the ten o'clock feed, Doreen was to go in as early as possible and get Danielle fed, bathed and dressed. Molly was going to drop the tin of milk powder before she had mixed the feed for her baby.

Mavis Clampton would have to go to the store cupboard in the kitchen to get more powder. Doreen would wrap

Danielle up in her large woolly cardigan and get out of the nursery as soon as Mavis disappeared into the kitchen.

Molly would put a rolled up blanket from the baby cupboard in Danielle's cot to make it look as though the child was in her cot. Margot would leave the nursery at the same time as Doreen as she was going to town that day.

Hopefully Mavis would be so concerned telling Molly off for making such a mess that she wouldn't notice the missing baby.

Marion was happy to help but was worried about Rosalind. So Annie said she would deal with her.

Doreen was very nervous and didn't sleep very well. Annie had told her the plan in their bathroom while they were supposed to be cleaning their teeth.

"They want me to sign the adoption papers tomorrow so it's got to be tomorrow. If Danny doesn't come, I will get on the bus and go to my Gran's."

The plan went surprisingly well. Molly, who had turned up late, dropped the milk powder making a big mess. Most of the girls had almost finished feeding their babies by the time Mavis went to the kitchen, so she wasn't surprised when she returned to find that most of the girls were leaving or had left.

Annie had kept a pile of peelings hidden in the pantry as an excuse to go to the dustbins behind the nursery. She waited till she heard the commotion in the nursery and slipped out to the dustbins behind the laundry. She tipped all her rubbish and some from one of the bins all over the floor. She went to the laundry and asked Rosalind if she could come and help her.

"I find it hard to bend down at the moment, so please will you help me pick this mess up, I slipped and dropped my rubbish bag."

Rosalind seemed pleased to help Annie and together they started to clear up the mess. Annie started to chat to her so slowing up the clearing up.

Marion appeared from the laundry and gave Annie a thumbs up behind Rosalind's back.

"Can I help," she said.

"No this angel has helped me. Thank you, Rosalind."

Marion and Rosalind returned to their washing in the laundry and Annie returned to the kitchen to find Mary grumbling because Doreen had not appeared in the kitchen to do the washing up.

"I think she had a funny tummy earlier, she is probably on the toilet."

Annie said.

"Humph, well I hope she keeps away from me, the last thing I need is the runs.

Chapter 17

Margot arrived in town and went straight to the market square

Linda Spicer, Norma's aunt was serving a customer. Margot hovered at the side of her stall.

"Hello, dear, Norma is at school, she still loves it. Always got her head in a book these days."

"Mrs Spicer, I need to have a private chat with you, it is urgent." Margot put her hand on Linda's arm.

Linda realized Margot was agitated. *Poor mite, she is going to lose her baby soon,* she thought.

"Mick will you look after my stall for a while, I need to be off for a while."

Big Mick on the next stall was only too glad to help Linda, as she often looked after his stall while he went and picked up his kids from school.

Linda took Margot's arm and they went round to the market café.

"What is it, love, how can I help?"

Margot suddenly felt very sheepish, what if she was opening a hornets nest?

"I don't know if we have got this all wrong, but me and my friend Annie think there is something not right about Norma's baby. We were told that her baby was born dead, but Norma told me that she heard the baby cry when he was born. The day after Norma was taken to hospital there was an extra baby in the nursery. We were told that it belonged to one of the private patients who was too poorly to look after him. We checked on the private patients and they all seemed to have their babies and all of them and the fathers seemed to be white, whereas the extra baby seems to be of mixed race."

Margot still wondered if she should be here and felt very nervous about what she was implying.

"He has now been taken back up to the private ward and is in a tiny side ward. One of the nurses feeds and changes him, and no-one else seems to go and see him."

Linda looked horrified. "Are you saying that the baby could be Norma's?"

"We don't know but it seems odd that he appeared the day after Norma gave birth. Annie heard one of the midwives saying that he was going to be adopted soon, so we felt we had to say something to put our minds at rest. We could be very wrong, but after the baby goes it will be too late."

"I will speak to Henry, my husband. He will know what to do. He is a police sergeant as you know, but you are right to have told someone. We will say nothing about this to Norma."

"Please don't tell them in the house where the information came from as our lives will be made miserable," Margot pleaded.

"Leave it with me, love, this certainly should be investigated. Come round next week and I will let you know what Henry thinks we should do."

Relief filled Margot, as the responsibility was now passed to someone else.

Margot suddenly realized the time and knew she would have to run to catch her bus.

Chapter 18

As Doreen climbed through the laundry window, her heart was full of dread.

What if Danny didn't come? What if they discovered she was missing and came after her?

She ran down the back driveway clutching her precious daughter. When she got to the road, she peered round the corner to make sure none of the staff were going in or coming out of the main entrance.

She couldn't see Danny or a car parked so she walked along the pavement. Then a car pulled out of a side road came slowly along and pulled onto her side of the road.

Doreen hesitated, nearly turned away but the driver's door opened and her father got out.

"Dad, please don't make me go back in there!"

George Cooper took Danielle from his daughter and opened the rear passenger door.

"Get in, love, you are both coming home."

Doreen cried all the way home, where her mother and Danny were waiting.

Danny had taken his letter to George and Joyce and they had all sat down with Danny's father and talked for many hours.

"You and Danielle are going to live with us until you are stronger. Give us a chance to get to know our granddaughter. Danny, myself and his father are going to redecorate the house where his father lives and make it suitable for two princesses," George said.

"Your Dad will deal with the House and let them know we have collected you and Danielle," Her mother said as she sat cuddling the baby.

"Please don't tell them how I got out as that will get the girls into trouble."

Danielle was cooing in her grandmother's arm and even George was finding it difficult to take his eyes from the child.

Doreen was safely home.

When Margot rang the bell to be admitted to the house on her return from town, she was met by a stony-faced Agnes Dayton.

"When you left this morning, who else went out through the door?" she snapped.

"No one, Miss, Mary unlocked the door for me, she will tell you."

Agnes stomped back to her office, obviously not a happy bunny.

Margot went into the kitchen to find Annie washing the lunchtime dishes.

"I thought you were on light duties now? "Margot said.

"They can't find Doreen. I thought she was unwell with that tummy bug she complained of last night," she winked at Margot as she said it.

"We all have to go to the day room at five o'clock this afternoon; the dragon wants to interrogate us."

"That's enough of that talk, lady." Mary appeared from the walk-in larder, obviously having been listening to the girls' conversation.

At that moment, the front door bell rang and Grace Maggs, looking very flustered, appeared from the office. She went and unlocked the front door and found George Cooper on the doorstep.

Margot had been about to go up to her room to take her coat off, but held back just behind the kitchen door, as the girls were not allowed to be in the hallway if visitors were coming in or out. Mary, being nosy, sidled up to the doorway to listen to what was becoming quite a loud altercation at the door.

Agnes Dayton's office door flew open and she marched to the door.

"Ah, Miss Dayton, I was just telling this lady that my daughter is now at home with her family. I collected her this morning as we have decided that our granddaughter will not be given up for adoption. I will be grateful if you will assemble my daughter's possessions for me to collect tomorrow morning. I will also collect her maternity allowance book at the same time."

"Mr Cooper, if you will step into my office where we can discuss this most irregular situation. We have organized a suitable couple at a lot of cost to adopt Doreen's child."

"As no papers have been signed, this is not going to happen I will call tomorrow morning at 10 a.m. Do I need to bring my solicitor?"

George stepped back from the door. Agnes knew she was beaten.

"That will not be necessary," she mumbled.

The front slammed shut and Agnes retreated to her office.

At five o`clock, the girls were all waiting in the sitting room. Annie whispered to Margot that the adoptive parents for Molly's baby had arranged their visit for that week.

When Agnes followed by Grace entered the room, the girls went quiet. Mary from the kitchen came in also. Florence was already in the room, knitting quietly at the craft table.

"I want to know how Doreen managed to leave this house without permission. Which of you knew that she planned this? Nurse Clampton told me that she only left the nursery for a few minutes to collect more milk powder, after the powder was supposedly spilled. What do you know about this Molly, as you were the one who dropped the powder? And what happened while Clampton was out of the nursery?"

Molly looked Agnes straight in her eyes and said, "Yes I dropped the tin of milk powder. It was a mistake. I was too busy cleaning it up to notice what anyone else was doing."

"What about you, Margot?"

"I was going to town so I left about the same time as Nurse Clampton went over to the kitchen. We were all going about that time, only Molly still had to feed her babe as she was late getting down to the nursery. I think Doreen went just after me."

"Who let her out of the door, Mary says she only let you out."

"Yes that is right, but perhaps the door wasn't locked properly after I left."

Margot had no qualms about pushing the blame onto Mary as Margot had suffered a lot of abuse from Mary's tongue over the weeks she had been in the house.

It became obvious to Agnes that she was not going to get anything from the girls. They either knew nothing or were very good liars.

"The rules are the rules; I will not stand any nonsense from any of you."

With that Agnes left the room slamming the door in Grace and Mary's face.

All the girls were secretly delighted that Doreen had escaped.

Chapter 19

After Margot had left Linda in the market café, she went to the telephone box in the corner of the market. She phoned the police station and asked to speak to Henry her husband.

"Hello, love, what's the matter?" Henry knew that something must be up for Linda to contact him at work.

Linda repeated the conversation she had with Margot. Henry was thoughtful for a minute.

"What the girls are suggesting is an awful accusation and a crime. Let me run this past the Inspector. He is a family man, one of his daughters got in the family way last year. He and his wife are now helping to bring up the little girl. He wouldn't let his girl go to one of those 'mother and baby homes' as we wouldn't have done if we had known about Norma."

"Henry, I don't think we have much time as the girls think the baby is soon to be adopted." Henry heard the panic in Linda's voice.

"Leave it with me, love, I will go and see the Inspector now.

Police sergeant Spicer sat at his superior officer's desk, who had listened with interest to the story Henry told him.

"As I understand it, Henry, a child that is born dead after a normal gestation period has to be registered. Was the child registered?"

"Not that I know of, we took Norma into our home when she came out of hospital. My wife is related distantly to her waste of space mother. When we heard of her predicament, we contacted the council asked if they would let her come to us when she was released from hospital. They agreed as we have fostered a couple of kids for them in the past, and they know us."

Chief Inspector Rudge thought for a minute. This was not the first time there had been queries raised about this particular home. But nothing was ever proved.

"Was Norma's baby expected around the time he was born or was it early? There is a fine line between miscarriage and a dead birth; I will have to check the exact difference. My wife was a midwife in the infirmary, she will know. But because you say the child may soon be adopted, I think I will pay a visit to the house tomorrow. I will take PC Boswell with me; you are too close to this to be involved. I will keep you informed, Henry."

When Henry got home, he relayed his interview with Chief Inspector Rudge to Linda.

"I went to the Library today and got this book. It's all about two scientists who have discovered a way of finding out who your parents are. It's called dioxy something or other. DNA for short. It says they can take samples from the child and the mother to see if there is a match. Couldn't the girls do that then we can find out if the little one is our Norma's?"

"Look, luv, the Chief is going to the house tomorrow. He will ask to see the registration papers, birth certificate, etc. for the child. Don't get your hopes up there may be some perfectly good explanation regarding the baby."

But Linda worried that they may be too late. She also knew nothing must be said to Norma. A few times Linda had heard her shedding a tear and when Linda had gone into her room it was obvious that she cried herself to sleep cuddling a little blue teddy that Linda had put in her room.

"If only she had been able to keep her baby, then she would have had someone of her own to love, and we would have looked after them both." Linda had grown very fond of the girl.

Chapter 20

The following morning the girls got up and went to their work. Margot and Molly went to the nursery for the first morning feed. There was no conversation at all. The other girls covertly glanced across at Margot and Molly who after feeding and bathing their infants were unwrapping the new clothes that the adoptive parents had brought in for the two babies to be dressed in ready for collection.

The babies were laid back in their cots; the other girls went on ahead leaving Molly and Margot to say their goodbyes in private.

When the girls were in the dining room, they heard the front doorbell ring.

No one spoke as Florence who was on breakfast duty went to answer the door. There was a mutter of conversation in the hallway and Florence returned to the dining room.

"A personal visitor for Miss Dayton," she told the girls.

The girls sighed with relief as they knew Florrie wouldn't lie to them and if it had been any of the adoptive parents they would have all been herded upstairs out of sight while the new parents picked up the babies.

After they had finished eating, the girls all went to their designated jobs, Molly and Margot went up to the private wing to collect the private patient's breakfast trays. Marion and Rosalind went to the laundry. Annie and Sharon went to the kitchen. Sharon to do the washing up and Annie to prepare the vegetables for supper.

Suddenly there was a crash from the hallway. Margot came in with a tray from the wing holding a broken teapot

"Sorry, Miss Baines, the pot slipped off my tray," Margot said.

Mary rushed to the hallway and saw the puddle of tea right outside Agnes's office door.

"Quick, Annie, get a scrubbing brush and bucket and clean it up before Miss Dayton comes out, and scrub the stain well or it will leave a mark."

Annie struggled to get down on the floor and scrubbed at the stain on the stone slabs. She could hear raised voices coming from Agnes's room.

Agnes was saying, "The agreement was that the money is to be paid in cash, a cheque is not what was agreed."

Another raised male voice, "But this is the bank the Queen uses, I do not carry that amount of cash!"

"Then I am sorry, Mr Abdulla we will find other adoptive parents for the child."

Then a woman's voice, "No please, we will come back with the money…"

Mary came over at this point and picked up Annie's bucket, inspected the tea stain and left Annie to struggle to her feet.

As she walked back into the kitchen, she felt something run down her leg, her waters had broken and she had a distinct pain in her back. She had felt uncomfortable in the night but had ignored it. Mary saw the problem and shouted at Sharon to come and clear up the mess and took Annie into the medical room next to the kitchen and went to get one of the midwives.

The rest of the day was a blur to Annie, she felt sorry for not being there for Margot and Molly, but as labour pains became more intense her mind was elsewhere.

The evening before, after the girls had gone to their rooms, Molly had lain on her bed looking at the photos she had secretly taken of Dinah. Her beautiful blue eyes looked up at the camera, her little tufts of feathery fair hair sticking up on her head like fairy down. Molly's face had become wet with tears; she had this hard pain in her chest. She had wished that the next day would never come.

She had pulled the bedclothes over her head but knew sleep was a long way off.

Molly had thought about Jane and her baby, Jonathon, safely ensconced in their little semi with her husband. She hoped that James would settle down and not break Jane's heart. Molly hoped she had made the right decision in not telling Jane of James's past relationship with her.

She had tried to think how pleased her mother would be when she got home. It was going to be hard not to think of Dinah, but she had no other choice. She had eventually cried herself to sleep, holding Dinah's photos, exhausted by the emotion.

In the other bedroom, Margot had sat in the dark, on the side of her bed, rocking herself back and forth, her mind racing.

Would they love Sonny as she did? Would he cry for her?

Margot had slid to the floor onto her knees and laid her head on her bed and begged for help from God.

She hadn't realized she had spoken out loud. The other girls had been laying in their beds awake, being fully aware of Margot's anguish. They had all wondered if they should go to her. When they heard her speak, they all left their beds and gone to her, she was by then shivering on the floor.

They knew there were no words to comfort her so they had helped her back into her bed and the girls had stayed on her bed till in exhaustion Margot had closed her eyes. Annie had stayed on Margot's bed holding her hand till she was sure that her friend was fully asleep.

At the ten o'clock morning feed, all the babies were still in the nursery.

So Molly and Margot had a little more time with their babies.

Mavis Clampton told both mothers to be careful not to mark the new clothes they had dressed Sonny and Dinah in and told all the girls to hurry up with the feeding and changing.

This could only mean one thing – the adoptive parents were soon due to arrive.

After the feeds the girls were all told to go to their bedrooms. The girls who were working were also summoned to go upstairs. Margot and Molly's cases were outside their rooms and they were instructed to pack their belongings into them.

"We will tell you when to resume your chores. Just spend the time tidying your bedrooms. Margot and Molly will be leaving after lunch."

Nurse Clampton, although she came across as a hard-faced bitch most of the time, actually felt sorry for the girls on adoption days.

The girls all trooped upstairs to their rooms. Molly went to the window of her room. Margot joined her. Quietly the other girls crept across the landing to Molly's room. Rosalind was not too sure what was happening as this was the first adoption day she had experienced, but she went with Marion and Sharon.

Marion put a cardigan round Molly's shoulders as she sat glued to the window. Margot sat quietly on Molly's bed, Sharon took her hand.

The tension in the room was unbearable; no one said a word.

At the sound of a car on the gravel in the drive, Margot stood up and joined Molly at the window. A silver Bentley slowly came to a halt outside the front door. A very smart well-dressed man got out of the driver's door and a fair-haired woman stepped from the passenger door.

The man gave the woman a hug and she smiled, looking so happy.

They went up the grey stone steps and the girls heard the front door bell ring.

It was as though no one in the room could dare to breathe. The silence was church like.

After 15 minutes the man and woman emerged. In the woman's arms, was a bundle wrapped up in a pink shawl. The girls glanced at Molly. She said nothing, seemed frozen to the spot.

Quietly Florence Sampson had come into the room. She gestured to Marion, Sharon and Rosalind to return to their rooms. They left Margot sitting on Molly's bed. They all heard the car drive away.

The three girls sat on their beds. Marion was in tears, Sharon was trying unsuccessfully to read her book and Rosalind was completely bewildered by the emotions she was feeling.

About 30 minutes later there was an ear-piercing scream, which seemed to go on and on. The girls opened their door and saw Florrie struggling with Margot in the doorway to Molly's room.

"Stop them, stop them," Margot screamed. Florrie just held Margot. She then seemed to go limp and the girls rushed over and helped Florrie to get Margot onto her bed in their room.

Molly came into the bedroom and took Margot in her arms and rocked her gently in her arms. Florence sat on Marion's bed. Sharon, Marion and Rosalind were all crying.

After ten minutes in which no-one spoke, a calm seemed to come over Margot and she sat up, wiped her face and said to Molly, "Thank you."

She looked at Florrie and her roommates. "I will be alright, thank you for being there."

The girls were then told to return to their duties while Molly and Margot got their possessions together and packed their suitcases.

Their suitcases were in the hallway when the girls came to the dining room for their sandwich lunch. Florence was on dining room duties for which they were all glad. There was not a lot of conversation at the table while the girls pecked at the food, no one having much of an appetite.

The taxi arrived for Molly and Margot, as the girls were leaving the dining room and goodbyes were said. Agnes Dayton never bothered to be present when the girls were leaving, only Grace and Florence saw them to the door.

While this was happening Annie was still in the throes of labour.

Sharon, had been sent to replace Molly on the private wing, and was told at suppertime that Annie had just given birth to a baby boy.

Sharon ducked into the labour ward and quickly told Annie of the day's events.

"I am sorry I wasn't there for Margot and Molly, poor Margot, I should have been there for them."

Sharon didn't tell Annie all the truth about the parting from their babies as she knew Annie would be upset.

The next day Annie was told to go back to the laundry and take over the ironing duties. Rosalind was pleased to see Annie as she was on full washing duties now as Marion was in the kitchen on lighter duties as she was suffering from high blood pressure.

Annie missed Margot, but was glad that they had exchanged addresses to keep in contact once Annie was home.

Chapter 21

As Annie was leaving the nursery after the two o'clock feed on her first day back at work, the front door bell rang.

Annie dived into the kitchen out of sight. Fortunately Mary was in the garden having her after lunch cigarette.

Grace Maggs came out of her small office next to Agnes's and went to answer the door and was surprised to see a man and a uniformed police woman standing on the doorstep.

"Good afternoon, madam. I am Chief Inspector Rudge of the city police and this is WPC Boswell," he said as they both showed their identification.

"We would like to see the person in charge, who we believe is Agnes Dayton."

Grace was taken aback but stepped back to allow the officers to enter the house.

"Miss Dayton is not available, I am afraid," Grace said, knowing that Agnes was having her after lunch siesta in her sitting room. No one was allowed to disturb Agnes at this time of day.

"I am very sorry, but it is a matter of some importance and the car registered to Miss Dayton is sitting in the drive. I can get a warrant if necessary to find the answers to my investigation. So please go and get her now."

The Inspector was pushing it a bit with the threat of a warrant, but he didn't want to give Dayton the chance to cover up any evidence.

It was obvious to Grace that the inspector was not going to go away, so she showed the police officers into her small office.

Grace went along to Agnes's sitting room and tapped on the door.

"Miss Dayton," she called as she tapped again.

The door eventually opened and a very angry looking Agnes stood there glowering at Grace.

"What do you want, you know that I will not be disturbed, you stupid woman, can't you deal with anything without running to me?"

She was about to slam the door in Grace's face.

"It's the police, they are here, and they are demanding to speak to you now. They say they will get a warrant if you refuse to see them."

Agnes looked aghast.

She went back into her room and put on the jacket of her suit and followed Grace back to the office.

Annie had heard a lot of the conversation at the front door and wondered if the police had come about the 'extra baby.' Margot had told Annie that she'd spoken to Norma's aunty and had hoped that someone would look into the situation.

The previous day, before Annie had been released from the labour ward, she had crept into the little side ward to see if the 'extra' baby was still there. He had been there, still on his own.

Her own son was being taken down to the nursery so she had been able to take a quick look before the nurse came back.

Annie left the kitchen as she knew Mary would soon return from her smoke, and returned to the laundry. Her thoughts were troubled, but knew that now she had given birth she would soon be allowed to go to town and made up her mind to go and see Norma's aunt in the market.

In the office, Agnes was red in the face at being disturbed.

"What is all this about, officer? And I want to see your identification?" she demanded. "This is a private maternity hospital and I object to your unwarranted intrusion!"

"Miss Dayton, I am here because some doubts have been raised about your adoption procedures. I have spoken to the Adoption Society you have purported to use and some irregularities have come to light. And because of this the children's welfare officer, Miss White, is entitled to examine your records, premises and the children you are proposing to offer for adoption."

Turning to PC Boswell he instructed her to go to the front door and ask Miss White to come into the building.

Agnes was not a happy woman.

"What do you want to see? I should have been notified of your intended visit."

"Then, Madam, it wouldn't have been spot check and vital papers may not have been available. Please ask you colleague to inform your nursery nurses that the welfare officer is going to visit your nursery and that all the babies must be accounted for with their relevant papers, birth certificates, etc."

Agnes nodded to Grace who first went to the private wards up the stairs. She met nurse Croft and explained what was going to happen. As she was talking, Sister Green appeared.

"What do you want Maggs?" she asked rudely.

Grace repeated the message and Alice looked flustered.

"I am having the afternoon off, you and Brenda can deal with this," Alice said and disappeared into the little side ward.

"Humph, I didn't know she was off this afternoon." Nurse Croft did not seem very pleased at all.

Nurse Croft accompanied Carol White to the private wards to speak to the patients. After she had checked out her patients and seemed happy that all was as it should be, nurse Croft noticed Alice drive off down the drive in her Morris Minor, seemingly in a hurry.

Meanwhile, Agnes was not having a good day. She was collecting all the files of the last six months adoptions under the eye of PC Boswell.

Chief Inspector Rudge accompanied Carol White, over to the girl's nursery. Nurse Clampton waited nervously as they got to each child. Annie's baby son had not yet been registered, as he was only one day old. It was customary for the mother on her first trip to town to go to the registry office to register their child.

All seemed to be in order. The Inspector queried Carol about any child in a side ward, but she had not found one. There had been an empty cot in the small side ward but no baby, she reported.

The Chief Inspector and Carol returned to Agnes's office.

"I just need to go through these papers with you, Miss Dayton, to clear up these irregularities. But first of all I would like to visit your laundry facilities to check that the correct procedures are being carried out in that department," Carol told Agnes.

Agnes looked as though she would explode. Grace fully expected it, but Agnes, purple in the face, sat down at her desk and said, "I will have the desk in Miss Maggs's office cleared for you to do what you have to do. Maggs, go and clear your rubbish off your desk at once."

Annie had gone back to the laundry and had started doing the ironing. She went out to the washing lines to fetch some more washing in that was dry enough to iron. She heard a whimper coming from the garden. She went round by the bins and was surprised to see an old grey pram behind the rhododendron bushes. The noise was coming from the pram so she crept over to look inside.

The little 'extra' baby was wrapped up tightly in a blanket in the pram.

Annie loosened the blanket a little and the whimpering ceased. The little face looked up at her and almost smiled. She put her hand in and he wrapped his tiny fingers around hers.

"Who have we got here then?" Annie nearly jumped out of her skin.

She turned and saw the policeman and a woman standing behind her.

"I just heard him cry. I don't know why he is here. We call him the 'extra' baby as he doesn't seem to have his Mum with him." Annie either had to shut up or go the whole hog, she didn't know what to do. So she burst into tears.

"I think you had better tell what you know. There is no need to be frightened," the chief inspector put his hand on Annie's shoulder.

"Let's go into the laundry and talk."

Annie followed them into the laundry room after covering the baby back up loosely, he seemed to have closed his eyes and gone to sleep.

"If I say anything, I will get into trouble, and I have my son to think of," Annie was still in tears.

But Carol assured her that her son would be quite safe, and she would not come to any harm.

So Annie explained about Norma being told her that baby was dead. Norma had told Margot that she had heard the baby cry after he was born.

After Norma was taken to hospital an extra baby appeared in the nursery and then later he had been taken up to the side ward.

"I think he is going to be adopted very soon as I heard one of the nurses say so when I took my roommate up to the labour ward. Could he be Norma's baby do you think? Please don't tell Miss Dayton I have talked to you. You don't know what she is like!"

"It's alright, Annie, we will keep you and your mates' names out of our enquiries with Miss Dayton. You just carry on with your ironing and we will deal with it all, and please do not discuss this with anyone else. Can we trust you?"

The Chief Inspector and Miss White went back to the sleeping child in the pram. Carol White was very disturbed about what Annie had told them. She told the Inspector that she felt the child needed to be protected until his parentage was ascertained. She wheeled the sleeping infant back to the house and gently lifted him from the pram and took him inside to the girl's nursery. She asked the Inspector to send PC Boswell to the nursery, where she instructed the constable to stay with the child while she made some phone calls.

Chief Inspector Rudge had spoken to his Superintendent about the information that Henry Spicer had given him. The Super's first reaction was that it was not worth following up, until Inspector Rudge mentioned Agnes Dayton's name and the address of the house. It rang a bell and he phoned through to his desk sergeant who had been at the station for as long as he had and who had a fantastic memory for names. When he heard the name and address, he thought for a minute. "Yes, Guv, remember the couple who made a complaint about three years ago. They were trying to adopt a baby from that place and the woman in charge wouldn't let them have the baby until they paid an extortionate amount of money. When we questioned it, she came up with a list of expenses as long as your arm, none of which we could disprove. We weren't happy about it; she was a nasty old baggage!"

Superintendent Tomlinson recalled the case and had to agree it had been one they had all been suspicious about at the time.

So he had given the OK for the Chief Inspector to proceed.

Carol White went into Grace Maggs's office and asked to use her phone to make some arrangements for a placement for the baby.

Chief Inspector Rudge was taking a statement from Agnes regarding the 'extra' baby as even he had started to refer to the little chap.

Agnes was saying she knew nothing about the child and they would have to speak to Sister Green as she kept all the papers regarding the girls' babies.

"Well as we can't find any papers that relate to this child then I have no alternative but to remove him into the care of

80

the Welfare Department until the papers are found and his mother is interviewed."

Agnes became very angry.

"This is an outrage; this is a private nursing home. The adoptive parents are on their way here today. The papers have all been signed. Sister Green must have them. You cannot remove this child."

Grace Maggs was standing in the hall, not knowing what to do.

The front door bell sounded. Mary Baines came out of the kitchen and went to open the door.

She was completely unaware of the drama that had gone on as she had been having a smoke in the garden when the police had arrived.

She ushered two smiling people into the hallway.

An Asian man and a white woman, both very well dressed.

"This is Mr and Mrs Abdullah, they have come to collect their new baby."

Agnes Dayton went into her office and slammed the door shut.

Grace Maggs was at a loss, the situation was beyond her.

Chief Inspector Rudge took control and ushered Mr and Mrs Abdullah into Grace's office.

After a very uncomfortable interview the Abdullah's left the house, very disappointed and upset. They were going to consult their solicitor to find out what their position was regarding the aborted adoption.

The Chief Inspector went into Agnes's office uninvited and told Agnes that he wanted her and Sister Green to come to the police station in the morning to answer more questions after the papers they were going to take had been inspected.

Agnes readily agreed and she even seemed calmer at the prospect that they were all leaving. The Inspector gathered up the paperwork that Grace had placed in a folder for them.

Annie was very worried by what she had told the policeman and wasn't sure who the woman was. Rosalind had heard part of the conversation between Annie and the Inspector as she had been hanging out the washing on the lines.

"What is happening, Annie? I saw that midwife, the one with the ginger hair, come over into the garden pushing a grey pram. She didn't see me as I was hanging up the big sheets. She left the pram and ran back into the house."

"I am not supposed to say anything, Ros. But I will tell you later when I am able. It's better at the moment if you don't know too much."

Agnes did not reappear from her office, so Grace thought as she was supposed to be the deputy supervisor she had better make sure all was running smoothly.

She went to the kitchen to see that the supper was being prepared. Then she went along to the girls' sitting room and spoke to Florence.

"Is everything alright, Florence, there has been a bit of an upset and Miss Dayton appears to be unwell, so any problems come and see me."

The girls were beginning to come into the sitting room from their duties and all seemed satisfactory, although Annie seemed a bit worried.

When Grace got back to her office, she found Sister Croft waiting outside.

"Alice has not returned from her afternoon off, Miss Maggs, and there is a private patient on her way in. I have been on duty since six this morning. Have you checked on her room? Maybe she has dropped off to sleep."

"No, I haven't had time as one of the mother's has got a temperature and the doctor is coming to have a look at her."

Grace Maggs decided that she would have to go and rouse Sister Green herself.

As Grace approached Alice's bedroom, she was surprised to see the door open. Grace tapped the door and stepped inside. The wardrobe door was open and all the clothes had gone. She checked the chest of drawers and found the same thing. The suitcases that were usually under Alice's bed were also not there.

As Grace went down the stairs, Agnes's office door opened. Agnes looked awful.

"Can I get you a cup of tea, Miss Dayton?" Grace asked gently.

"I need more than tea, Grace, can you come to my sitting room for a minute or two?"

Grace was so surprised that Agnes used her Christian name, and meekly followed Agnes to her room where she was invited to sit down.

Agnes poured two glasses of sherry and offered one to Grace.

"I will be tendering my resignation, Grace, and I have recommended that you take over as superintendent."

Grace was astonished.

"I don't understand. Sister Green appears to have packed her things and gone!"

Agnes nodded her head, seemingly unsurprised.

She mumbled something like "Rats deserting the sinking ship" to herself.

"I haven't always been as kind to you as I should have, Grace, and I do not deserve any favours, but I will ask anyway. Will you wait until the morning before notifying the chairman of the managing committee of my decision?"

Grace thought for a moment and then said, "We have a pressing problem with Sister Green's absence, so I will have that to deal with this evening. So I will not have the time to make phone calls tonight."

"Thank you, Grace."

With that Agnes walked out of her room and went up the stairs.

Grace then returned to her office and found the number of the nursing agency that they used to get a temporary replacement midwife to cover for that evening.

She then went up to find Sister Croft and ask her if she would stay until the agency midwife arrived. She knew that

Florence had done some nursing so she went and spoke to her to ask if she could assist for the evening.

The evening went well, Florence spent the night on the private wing with Sister Croft; the private patient's baby was delivered in the early hours. The girls had gone up to their rooms aware that there had been something going on. Annie still worried about her conversation with the policeman, but eventually all was quiet in the house.

As Grace was getting undressed just before midnight, she wasn't surprised to hear Agnes's car drive off down the gravel drive. She did wonder if she should have rung the police station, but decided to pretend she had heard nothing and wait and see what the morning brought.

Chapter 22

Annie was to go to town the following day to register the birth of her son. At breakfast, Grace Maggs had come into the dining room and told the girls that Miss Dayton had resigned. She made the excuse that Dayton was ill, and that for the time being she would be acting as Superintendent until the managing committee made a new appointment.

The girls were delighted as were the staff when she had called a staff meeting prior to speaking to the girls.

Grace had also telephoned the Chairman of the management committee and explained that Agnes Dayton had resigned and left the house along with Sister Green.

The Chairman had already been contacted by Superintendent Tomlinson of the City Police earlier that morning so was aware of the investigations that were taking place.

It appeared that the police and welfare were convinced that Miss Moggs had nothing to do with the irregularities being investigated.

Therefore The Chairman confirmed to Grace that he was happy for her to take over Agnes's position for a temporary period until the committee had met to discuss the situation.

After lunch Annie got on the bus to go to town. She went to the Registry office to register Simon's birth, then she went to the market to find Linda, Norma's aunt.

As Annie hadn't been to the city before, she had to ask where Mrs Spicer's stall was. Fortunately it was Big Mick she asked, he was standing at the burger van near the entrance to the market.

He told her that Linda had taken the day off as she had some business to attend to.

So a disappointed Annie went to the bus stop to return to the house.

Linda and Henry were actually at the police station. They had been summoned by Chief Inspector Rudge. They were both keen to hear of any results of the police visit to the house, which Henry knew had taken place the day before.

"Thank you, Mrs Spicer and Henry, for coming in especially on your day off, Henry. As you know, I visited the house yesterday afternoon with WPC Boswell. We took Carol White, the children's welfare officer with us.

At first, Miss Dayton refused to see us but I leaned on her a bit and eventually she condescended to speak with us.

Carol checked all the paper work on the resident babies and found they had all been registered except one that had only been born the day before. The private patients and their offspring were all present and correct."

Linda looked a bit upset, "So that means that the little one, that Margot told me about has got his mother with him?"

"We couldn't find a child in a side ward as you were told, Carol did find an empty cot. It wasn't until we went over to inspect the laundry facilities that we found a baby in a pram hidden behind the bushes in the garden. Annie had heard the child whimper and was comforting him. She confirmed that this was the 'extra baby' as they have always called him"

"Oh my goodness, poor little scrap, you haven't left him there have you?"

"No, Carol has removed him from the home as we cannot find any papers that relate to him. He is in the care of the welfare department for the time being."

Both Henry and Linda looked very relieved.

"Another development that I don't want you to speak of to anyone. I probably shouldn't even tell you, but as you are a serving police officer Henry you will no doubt become aware of these developments.

The nursing Sister at the house left the house with all her belongings within an hour of our visit, Agnes Dayton has also disappeared in the night also with all her belongings. She told her deputy that she was resigning and was gone by this morning."

"So there has been some 'jiggery pokery' going on then. But at least the little lad is safe now. So what happens now, Guv?"

"As I understand it, there is a procedure that can determine the parentage of a child. The welfare would like to take a sample from your foster daughter to see if there is a match with the child.

I suggest at this stage the girl is not made aware of the need for this, as she has been through a huge trauma in losing her child as it is. Perhaps you could concoct a little white lie to allow this test to happen without raising the girl's hopes."

Linda and Henry agreed that this should be done as soon as it was possible.

"What is going to happen about those dreadful women from the home, I don't understand why they would take a child away like that."

Neither Henry nor Linda could understand the motive behind what had happened.

"Soon after our arrival a couple came to the house and we believe they were hoping to adopt the little chap. They had been told to bring 'the expenses' money in cash. It was a large sum, but they were prepared to pay as they wanted a child of mixed race as the husband was Asian and his wife white. They wanted to pass the child off as their own. They hadn't wanted to go through a regular adoption agency and were prepared to pay for a very private, no questions asked adoption.

We believe that several of the adoptions were conducted in this manner. Not through the official channels with large amounts of money exchanging hands. They will all be thoroughly checked out."

"My God will you be able to catch those women?" Linda asked.

"I am sure everything will be done to bring them to court, meanwhile we must go and sort out this sample taking with our Norma," Henry said.

"I will arrange for the doctor to call round to your house about tea-time tonight. Is that all right? We need to get this sorted out as soon as possible for all concerned," the Chief Inspector said.

"We will tell Norma that I am taking part in a test for medical research and ask her to participate, they can do me as well so that she doesn't realize it is her we need to test."

"Yes that's a brilliant idea; she was on about being a blood donor to help other people so I am sure she will be willing to do this," Henry said as they went out of the police station.

Chapter 23

Grace had asked Florence to take on the role as her deputy until the new appointments were made by the committee.

The whole atmosphere in the house changed. The work was still hard but the girls were allowed to talk to each other in the sitting room and were encouraged to speak to Florence or Grace if they had a problem.

Their letters were no longer read before posting or incoming. Family visitors were encouraged and even sour-faced Mary in the kitchen managed a smile now and then.

The time was approaching for Sharon's baby to be adopted. Grace talked to Sharon, when it was time to sign the adoption papers, even giving her a cup of tea while they sat together in her office.

Sharon cried and told Grace that she had secretly written to her father and Mother telling them that she wanted to keep Dominic her baby. But had received no reply.

"Sharon, a letter did come to the house from your father in response to your letter. I kept it, as Miss Dayton would have wanted to know how you had been able to send a letter to your parents without her knowledge. Your father's letter was addressed to Miss Dayton. He was adamant that in no circumstances would he or your mother allow you to return home with a child. We were instructed to tell you, that your parents would disown you and the child and all your allowances would be terminated if you kept the child."

Sharon was devastated. But part of the old selfish Sharon was conflicting with the love for her child. She did enjoy being the spoilt daughter with everything at her feet. Her parties, her circle of rich friends, and if her father cut her allowance off, how would she be able to support Dominic?

Grace could see the mental conflict going on in her head.

"A new family for Dominic, with lots of love is what an adoption would give him. If you keep him, you will have to get a job and find somewhere to live, unless his father would support you?"

Sharon laughed, "If I knew which one was the father," she said trying to lighten the situation.

"No, Miss Maggs, you are right, I want to go back home with no regrets. Give me the adoption forms and let's get it over with."

Grace was not surprised, as she had heard Sharon's comments throughout her pregnancy and although she had seemed to have bonded with her child, Grace knew that the girl wouldn't cope financially or emotionally on her own.

The selfish Sharon was still uppermost.

The papers were signed and adoptive parents were being sort.

Annie's son, Simon, was the next child about whom an adoption decision had to be made.

Annie had no intention of parting with Simon.

When Grace called Annie into her office to discuss this, it soon became clear that Annie's mind was made up.

Annie told her that whatever her parents or Simon's father said, her child was not going to be adopted.

Grace was worried that when Annie left the house she would have nowhere to go. Annie's parents and the other grandparents had made their views very clear when she first came to the house.

Grace decided to write to both sets of parents and put them in the picture. The replies she received a few days later, were still very negative.

So Grace tried again to talk to Annie.

"I have tried to alter your parent's minds about you returning home with your son, but to no avail. I am not sure what to advise you."

"Miss Maggs, I have seen an advert in the *Family* magazine. This woman is looking for a girl to help her look after her grandson, and the advert says that someone with a child would be considered."

Annie gave Grace the magazine.

'Help required in London home. Duties include looking after a two-month-old baby and household duties. Woman with child considered.'

"Well it looks all right, but will you allow me to make some enquiries first. Would you allow me to do that?"

Annie agreed and the matter was left in Grace's hands to contact the advertiser for more information. Grace had an old friend who lived in London and she decided to ask her to visit the address after she had made contact.

Sharon meanwhile was becoming more withdrawn and the moments she spent with Dominic became precious. She tried to put up a 'don't care' attitude, but the girls could see through her bravado.

Annie always went and sat with Sharon and Marion after they had finished their chores, as they were the last two left from the original roommates. The new girls who had come in since Margot and Molly had left were in Molly's old room and kept to themselves.

Sharon wouldn't talk about the forthcoming adoption and Annie didn't discuss her plans with either of them.

Sharon knew that the experience of being in the house had changed her.

She had got to know her own weaknesses, she was a selfish cow. The thought of being tied to someone wholly dependent on her was terrifying. At times, she felt guilt but then the thought of being home again, back in her old life overruled any feelings of guilt. Plus she kept telling herself Dominic would have a proper family who would give him all that she felt she was incapable of.

When the adoption day came, the girls as usual were sent to their rooms. The new girls in Molly's old room were surprised when Sharon and the others came into their room.

When the car, another top of the range vehicle, came up the drive, Sharon withdrew from the window and sat on the bed. As the car drew away, Sharon got up and left the room, no tears, no hysterics, but the pain was obvious.

Half an hour later her case packed, she said a quiet goodbye to Annie and Marion. She shook's hands with Grace and Florrie. Her father arrived shortly after and without a backward glance she left the house.

It upset Annie and Marion just as much as if she had screamed. The pent up emotion was there absorbed in Sharon's sad eyes and enforced calm.

"It would have been better if she had cried and let it out, the hurt could fester and destroy her," Annie said.

The two girls hugged each other and wept for Sharon.

Chapter 24

Henry Spicer asked the police doctor, as he let him into their house, that evening if he would take a sample from Linda first, so as not to arouse any suspicions in Norma's eyes as to the real reason the swabs were being taken. The doctor was fully aware of the situation and was happy to oblige.

"Norma has no idea that her baby may be alive, and we could all be mistaken so we don't want to raise her hopes. We know she has a little cry at night sometimes, about the baby, so to lose him a second time would be too cruel."

The procedure was done very quickly and Norma thought it all rather fun, especially as she thought she was taking part in scientific research.

Linda had bought Norma a new record and she quickly went up to her room to listen to it quite happily, after the doctor left.

Chief Inspector Rudge was not surprised that Agnes Dayton and her obvious partner in crime had done a 'bunk' as he put it.

The records he had taken showed quite a few financial discrepancies, and it was clear that quite a few of the adoptions had been covered by large 'donations ', as it was described in the accounts , plus expenses.

Agnes had withdrawn a large sum from her bank account as had Sister Green, the day following their disappearance from the house. The accounts had since been frozen. It was believed there had been other accounts stripped of assets which the police had not been able to discover until too late.

Both women had managed to disappear very quickly and it was assumed that the escape plan was something set up in case their misdemeanours were ever discovered and a quick 'flit' became necessary.

Two women matching their descriptions had been seen at Heathrow airport on the closed circuit cameras the evening after they left the house.

These two females had boarded a plane to South America.

The Chief Inspector would have loved to bring the two women to book, but extradition from South America was a costly procedure and as the Superintendent had pointed out at least they wouldn't be fleecing anymore adoptive parents plus the fact that they had saved the 'extra baby' as he was still called.

The following week Grace called Annie into the office. I have received an answer from the lady who put the advertisement in the magazine. I also asked a friend of who lives in London to visit the house. It seems that the position is genuine.

All we have to do is get your parents' permission, as you are only 18 and without their permission you cannot take the position.

"I will not give Simon up, Miss Maggs. If my parents refuse, then they will never see me again and I will accept the position without their permission."

Grace could see that Annie would not change her mind, so after Annie had left she sat down to write again to Annie parents.

She explained that Annie was adamant that she would not give her son up, and told the parents about the living-in position that Annie wanted to take. Then she wrote…

'Allowing your daughter to take this position would allow her to provide for her son, your grandson.

'She is sad that you won't allow her to return home with Simon, who is a bonny baby, but Annie will not be persuaded to part with him.'

Grace thought that to remind Annie's parents that the child was their grandson may jolt their conscience.

She sealed up the letter with no great hope that it would do any good.

The following Monday, Annie went to town again. She went straight to the market and found Linda, who was pleased to meet her. Margot and Norma had told Linda about Annie, and she knew that they had her and Margot to thank for protecting the 'extra baby'.

Linda left her stall for Big Mick to mind, and they went round to the café.

Linda told Annie that she must not repeat anything that she told her.

The swabs were being tested by the police forensic scientists and the results would soon be known. But Norma had no idea that her baby may still be alive.

Annie was pleased to hear that there was a possibility that the 'extra baby' could be Norma's lost child.

"Please can you let me know what happens? I will be leaving the house very soon as my son will be six weeks old shortly…"

Annie told Linda about her plans and that she hoped her parents would not put a stop to her going to London. She took Linda's address in case she couldn't get back into town before she had to leave the house.

When Annie got back to the house, she was told that Marion had gone into labour and by the morning they were all told that she had a baby boy.

The reply came back very quickly from Annie's parents. Grace was pleased to read that they had no objections to her taking the job in London.

Annie wrote immediately to Simon's father and his letter arrived by return post saying that he would come to Yorkshire and take her and Simon to the job in London. He was pleased that Annie had stood her ground over their child, he had tried many times to speak to his parents about bringing Annie and his son home, but his parents had refused to discuss the matter.

A week later Philip arrived to take Annie and Simon away from the house.

Although she was glad to be leaving, she was sad at leaving Marion. She also had become very fond of Florence. Marion was allowed to come to the front hall along with Florence and Grace to say goodbye. After a quick hug from Marion she went to shake hands with Florrie who ignored her out stretched hand and gave Annie a big hug.

"Please let us know how you get on, Annie, and take care." Annie could have sworn there was a tear in Florrie's eye.

Grace shook her hand and wished her all the best.

They climbed into the taxi that Philip had arrived in. Annie looked at the driver and he smiled. It was the same man that had brought her here five months earlier. It seemed that she had gone in a full circle.

The driver gently took Simon while she climbed in the car, he then loaded the big blue case into his boot and without a backward glance they left the house behind.

Chapter 25

So Annie went to London with baby Simon.

Six weeks later, Marion went through the trauma of signing the adoption papers and then watching her son's new parents come and take him away.

Sharon had returned to her old life with her parents. But a much more serious girl had gone home. She had learned a very hard lesson and was very much more aware that thoughtless actions have consequences which cast very long shadows.

Doreen and her boyfriend were doing fine. Coping with a child, they were learning, was a full time job, but Doreen's parents were always on hand and they all adored Danielle.

Molly had returned home to her mother, but was a much saddened girl. Her mother's delight at having her daughter home helped Molly. Although her mother was very frail, she was strong in spirit and hadn't deteriorated in her illness since Molly had been away.

Although Molly had Jane's address, she rarely communicated with her friend. She didn't want to be invited to visit. Jane seemed to understand as seeing Jane with her child could bring back memories of her loss of Dinah.

In truth, Molly would have liked to see Jane's little boy as he was a link to Dinah, but the thought of bumping into Jane's husband made the decision an easy one.

Margot had gone home in a very bad state. She tried hard to put the whole incident out of her mind. Her mother had found the photos of Sonny Jim and had hidden them away, hoping this would help Margot to forget. After a week or so her depressed state did not improve. Her mother took her to the doctor who was aware of what had taken place. The doctor was concerned for Margot's mental state and had prescribed pills which he asked her mother to administer.

Eventually, Margot seemed to be coping better and the doctor thought it would be a good idea for her to return to work to take her mind off the past.

Her mother saw an advert in the local bakers for an assistant and Margot applied. She got the job and soon found she was enjoying life a little more.

Two weeks later, Norma's foster parents received a letter from the welfare authorities saying they would like to come to the house and see them also Norma.

Norma stayed at home on the day of the visit, she was a little frightened that the welfare department were going to move her to a new foster home. The Spicer's told her not to worry but were afraid to say more. Henry had taken a few days of his annual holiday and so was also at home.

When Henry opened the front door, he was surprised not only to see Carol White, the welfare officer but also Chief Inspector Rudge.

"Morning, Guv, and Miss White, please come in."

Linda made some tea and they all sat in the Spicer's front room.

"Hello, Norma, you must be wondering why I have come to see you all," Carol said.

"It was very sad about your baby, what did you feel about it?"

"Well, Miss, I don't know nothing about babies but I would like to have seen him."

"The people in charge at the house were not very nice people, Norma, and the other girls were all very sad about what happened to you. The girls thought there was something not quite right the night you had your baby. You were taken to hospital and the baby stayed at the house. You were told that the child had died, but two of the girls still thought there was something wrong. Over the next few weeks they were convinced that they should tell someone about their concerns.

"Before Margot left, she told Mrs Spicer of their suspicions and Sergeant Spicer spoke to Chief Inspector Rudge. Enquiries were made as there had been previous complaints about the happenings at the house."

"What are you saying, Miss, I don't understand?" Norma was looking puzzled.

"There was an extra baby in the girl's nursery the day after you were taken to hospital, Norma. As Miss Dayton could not produce any registration papers for this child, the baby was taken into the care of the welfare department.

Do you remember the test we took from you over a week ago, we also did the same test on the baby. The test told us that this child was your little one and therefore he did not die as you were told. Your little son is alive and well!"

Norma burst into tears and Linda took her into her arms.

"Please can I go and see him, please Aunty Lin can we go and see him. They will let me see him, won't they?"

Tears were running down Linda's face as she clutched the shaking girl. Even Henry's eyes filled.

"Look, love, if Miss White and her department are agreeable your little son can come here and live with us. But the final decision is yours. Either you can allow me and Uncle Henry to help you look after him or if you want him to be adopted we will support you, it is your decision."

Norma was still shaking and turned to Henry and said, "Please can he come home? He could be a policeman like you and he wouldn't get into trouble like I did."

Carol White had envisaged this possible outcome and had run it past her department and knew that there would be no objection to this happening.

"I don't think this solution would be refused if everyone wanted this to happen," Carol said.

"Please can we go and see him," Norma said going to fetch her coat.

"Your son is actually waiting outside in the car with my colleague and is eager to meet his mummy."

"Well, Miss White, you had better bring the little man into his new home," Henry said.

Carol went to the front door and beckoned to the nursery nurse who was waiting patiently in the car outside.

Norma rushed to the door and the sleeping child was brought in and put into her arms. She walked into the room and sat down on the settee next the Linda. She could not take her eyes off the infant, who opened his eyes and everyone watching would have sworn he smiled up at his mother as he curled his tiny fingers around Norma's.

There wasn't a dry eye in the house even the Inspector had to blink back a tear.

"What are you going to name him, Norma?" Linda asked.

"At school, we have been learning about William the Conqueror and I thought that if my baby had lived I would have called him William, but now he really is a conqueror, he will be William Henry after you, uncle. We will call him Billy, is that alright?"

Henry was choked; he was very touched.

Chapter 26

The house was no longer a Mother and Baby Home or a private nursing home. The views on unmarried pregnancies had also changed. It no longer carried the awful social stigma that it did in 1960. Contraception was more prominently advocated and family planning clinics were becoming part of the norm.

Of course there were still girls getting pregnant but it was dealt with in a more humane way. Condom machines began to appear in toilets and the pill was becoming more available. Parents were more inclined to support their daughters now and help them rather than send them away. There were still a few mother and baby homes, but a more sympathetic approach was adopted and legislation demanded that mothers had support and advice.

Margot still lived in her parents rented house. Her father had died three years after Margot had Sonny Jim adopted. She still worked in the bakers shop. She really enjoyed the work and had even taken on some of the baking.

Her mother now in her nineties was still active in her mind but not her body. So Margot's free time was spent cooking all the meals and household chores. The only outing Margot had was to wheel her mother to church on a Sunday.

The vicar called in every week to see Violet, Margot's Mum, and had a great admiration for the devoted way Margot looked after her mother. His visits usually coincided with Margot's afternoon off from the shop.

Violet often teased Margot saying that the vicar was only coming to see Margot not her.

"Don't be daft, Mam, he is only doing his vicar thing," she would say.

The baker's shop was only a short distance from their home, so Margot could pop back at lunchtime to give her mother her lunch.

The grocery shop where she had worked before Sonny was born was now under new ownership. Sonny Jim's father had been killed in a motorcycle accident soon after Margot returned home and his family had sold up and moved away. Although sad, Margot was relieved not to have to face that family again.

Her father's comment at the time had been, "God doesn't pay his debts in money, love."

Margot had found Sonny's photos that her mother had put out of sight. She would look at them now and again and try and picture what he would look like now. Every year on his birthday she would have a little weep, her mother knew but said nothing.

On the afternoon of Sonny's thirtieth birthday, Margot was sitting in the back yard, as it was her day off. She was as usual wondering where her son was and hoping that he was well, as she gazed at the now faded photographs that Molly had managed to take.

As usual, the tears were running down her face.

A hand came down on her shoulder. Margot didn't look up, as she knew it would be her mother.

"Oh, Ma, it doesn't get any easier, I hope God is looking after him."

"Margot, what is it, my dear?"

Margot jumped up from her seat, stuffing the photos into her apron pocket.

"Vicar! I am fine thanks."

"Margot, please let me help. Who is the baby in the photos?"

"No one Mr Granger, I am fine, just being silly."

Margot went back into the kitchen to put the kettle on for the vicar's usual cup of tea.

"Margot, please sit down and please not Mr Granger, my name is Peter. I have a high regard for you and have been hoping that we could become friends. I had intended to ask you today if you would consider allowing me to take you out to tea on your next afternoon off. But seeing you so upset I think you need a friend today."

Margot realized Peter was holding her hand. The kindness of his tone and his look of concern were too much for Margot on this very emotional day.

She sat down and wept, once the tears had subsided she thought, *if I tell him he won't want anything to do with me.*

"Who is the baby, Margot, was he yours?"

Margot nodded, she knew it was too late to lie.

"He had to be adopted." That awful word, she had given her child away.

Peter could see the pain in Margot's eyes.

He went to the kettle and made the tea. Poured out a cup for her mother and took it into the sitting room then came back and poured two more.

"Now Margot, please tell me all about this lovely child?" He removed Sonny's photos from Margot's pocket and laid them on the table.

So Margot told Peter her story, fully expecting him to run for the hills.

But that didn't happen. Peter started take Margot out every week and she began helping in the church when she could leave her mother.

Violet was delighted about the situation as she was quite a sick woman and was glad that Margot would have someone to care for her when she was no longer in this world.

Violet passed away a couple of months later, Peter was a tower of strength to Margot spending most evenings with her when he wasn't attending to his pastoral duties.

Peter and Margot were married six months later. Margot was so happy and threw herself into church events. Peter had

Sonny's photos put into a beautiful frame and it held pride of place in the vicarage sitting room. Anyone who asked was proudly told it was Margot's son.

Nearing Sonny's next birthday Peter said to Margot," I was speaking to John Hannay this morning and he was telling me about one of his cases. It was regarding a mother who wanted to trace a child that she had adopted some years ago. The interesting part was that he told me that the law has recently changed regarding adopted children. Apparently now it is much easier to trace a child than it was. I wonder, is this something that you would like to consider my darling?"

Margot had often dreamed of finding Sonny. She often looked at young men of a similar age to Sonny and wondered if they could be her son. But then her mind would argue: would it be fair to try and find her boy?

Yes she longed to hold her boy and tell him she had never forgotten him, but would he forgive her for abandoning him?

"No pressure, darling, I just thought you may like to consider it!

Peter was the kindest of husbands and adored Margot. He knew she still shed a tear every now and then. But if they found the boy and he refused to see his mother this would only make things worse. The whole thing needed careful consideration and whatever happened Margot would need his full support.

Peter decided to speak to his friend John again. He was a solicitor and had a lot of experience in family matters. Peter didn't mention it again to Margot. He thought if he could find a way forward without stressing Margot out, he was willing to try.

Doreen had moved out of Danny's father's house and now lived in a council house closer to her parents who were retired but still in good health. She had given birth to a baby brother to Danielle 18 months after she had left the house. Danielle was now married and had made Doreen a grandmother.

Her relationship with her children's father had failed soon after her son was born. Doreen got suspicious when Danny

104

started staying out late at night and she found lipstick on his collar.

When challenged, Danny admitted that he had met someone else. Doreen packed his bags and they were divorced within that year.

Doreen applied for a council house and had been allocated a house near to her parents. She had soon settled in and within the year she had remarried the son of her next-door neighbour. The two children liked there step-dad and Doreen was happy. She often thought about the sadness that she had seen in the 'house' and wondered what had happened to her roommates but she hadn't taken any contact numbers and so she would now never know.

Molly, now 53 years old had looked after her mother, for three years after she had returned home. Her mother had deteriorated very quickly with a form of dementia in her last year. Molly had promised her mother that she would never put her in a home. It had been very hard but it helped to put thoughts of Dinah to the back of her mind.

After her mother passed away Molly decided that she would like to work in the museum. A friend had told Molly a lot about the work and it had captured Molly's imagination. She had gone to college and studied for a curator's qualification, which she passed easily. She had worked in the local city museum now for over 20 years and was highly respected for her knowledge of the exhibits. She had been the senior curator now for the last seven years.

Molly had a nice circle of friends but never let anyone get too close. Her heart was closed to deep emotion she preferred light relationships. Her photos of Dinah were fading and dog-eared and her most precious possession. She had never shown them to anyone.

Molly always sent Jane a birthday card. She would put in a short note each time to Jane telling her a little about her working life.

Jane would also send a birthday and Christmas card to Molly, always being careful to avoid saying too much about Jonathon and never mentioned the past.

Her thoughts of Dinah were never too far away from her mind but she had trained herself to steer herself in other directions especially when Dinah's birthday came around.

There were four other members of staff in the museum. Two male and Hilary a lady nearing to retirement. The two men were Frank and David. Frank had tried repeatedly to get Molly to go out for a meal with him but had soon realized she wasn't interested. David was a nice chap, he lived with his male partner and was one of the kindest people Molly had ever met.

Molly knew that Hilary was looking forward to her retirement and she would soon have to advertise for a replacement. Hilary had told her she would wait until a replacement had been found so Molly had typed up an advert to send to the local paper.

Molly hoped that someone with a real interest in the artefacts in the museum would apply, not someone who just wanted any job.

The week following the advert appearing in the paper Molly received several applications. She interviewed three promising candidates. Two men and one female. She took each candidate around the museum and watched how interested they seemed in the exhibits. Both the men walked around and listened to Molly's description of the contents of the cabinets. The girl asked many questions and seemed keen to learn more, so Molly decided to offer her the post.

Hilary had dealt with the written application forms and was pleased that Molly had chosen the girl.

"I think she will be an asset to the museum," said Hilary.

Her name was Emily Johnson.

Jane and her family had just come back from a holiday in Spain. Jonathon her son was now living in London with his wife and two children. So they thought it would be nice to have a holiday together. They had rented a villa in one of the

Costa's and had spent a week in the sun. It had all been lovely to spend time with her grandchildren.

James her husband hadn't been all that enthusiastic about the holiday, but had been persuaded by his son to at least go for one week.

Jane was pleased to be back home as James had been his usual flirty self with every barmaid or waitress they had seen. Even Jonathon had told his father to behave a couple of times. James had been drunk nearly every night and had snored loudly all night and some evenings not even bothering to accompany the family out of the villa.

When they arrived back in London, Jane and James stayed one night with Jonathon and his wife before catching the train north to Yorkshire in the morning.

Jonathon asked his mother if everything was all right between his parents.

"Yes, darling, he is always the same after a drink or two. I take no notice; it's his liver he is destroying. It's been so lovely to spend some time with you all. Perhaps next time I will come down on my own."

Jane wasn't going to tell Jonathon that her and James lived virtually single lives. He spent most evenings at the golf club, or that's what he told Jane. When he was at home, they hardly had any conversation, often just grunting when she spoke to him. Basically Jane had given up and had joined a chess group and several craft groups. She also volunteered in a cancer charity shop which she enjoyed. She was nearly always in bed before James came home and he had taken to sleeping in another bedroom.

At fifty-three years old, the need for a physical relationship was not all that important to Jane, but when she watched a romantic film, she often felt very lonely and unloved.

As the train thundered northwards, Jane's thoughts went to Molly.

"I ought to go and see Molly, perhaps we can have lunch one day, and it's only about an hour's drive. I will find her telephone number and give her a ring and see if she will agree to a meet up," Jane decided.

She hadn't actually seen Molly since she had left the house and apart from the yearly cards they hadn't spoken.

It is time! Jane, thought.

Jane was pleased to get back to her routine at home. Her half days in the charity shop were a pleasure, her colleagues were pleased to see her back.

They had all realized that Jane's home life was not particularly happy, but she was always so pleasant to the customers and the other volunteers who helped in the shop.

There was a chess match at the club she belonged to and a craft fair to arrange that month so Jane's intended phone call to Molly was put on hold for the time being. So life continued in the same old way.

Chapter 27

Annie had settled into her new job in London. Philip had got to know his little son on the long train ride south and was even more determined to talk the parents round to allowing Annie and Simon to come home.

He had said he would visit every weekend to see them both but this turned out not to be possible. Annie's household duties turned out to be more intense than she had imagined, plus she was expected to work from nine to five in her benefactor's corner shop.

Her day started at six in the morning when she had to feed, bath and dress Mrs Gates grandson and Simon. Do the laundry and hang it onto the line, grab a quick breakfast of cereal and then dash down to the shop for nine o'clock. This was six days a week. She had to run back during her lunch break to feed and change both children, then be back in the shop by two.

In the evening, before she had her dinner, cooked by Mrs Gates, she had to see to both babies. After dinner she would have all the ironing to do.

Neither Simon nor David the grandson were good sleepers, so during the night she was often walking the floor with one or the other baby.

Annie was always so tired.

On Sundays, both babies were put in the pram after the mid-morning feed and Annie had to walk them around Hampstead Heath as Mr and Mrs Gates always had friends calling in for lunch on Sundays. Annie was given two bottles ᴑr the babies and a pack of sandwiches for her and told not to return till after four in the afternoon.

A dried up plate of a Sunday lunch was left for her after she had settled the children, Usually Mrs Gates would then produce a pile of her husband's shirts for Annie to iron before she went to bed.

Annie received no payment for any of the shop work, but food and toiletries were provided.

After a month, Philip came up to see Annie. He was appalled at the weight Annie had lost. He had tried to come sooner but Mrs Gates had kept telling him that it wasn't convenient.

So without asking, knowing Annie's Sunday routine from her letters, he was waiting outside as she and the two babies left the house for their usual perambulations around the Heath.

He was appalled at the weight she had lost, and spent the afternoon planning what he was going to say to his and Annie's parents on his return home.

He had taken his Brownie camera with him and took photos of his son and managed to get a couple of an unwilling Annie, which when developed he took to her parents and his own. Annie's father was dismayed. Her mother still afraid of 'what the neighbours would say', took a little persuading, but her heart was touched by the photos of Simon and her poor thin worn down daughter.

They arranged with Mr and Mrs Gates to visit. Annie was given the day off from the shop and Mrs Gates went to great pains to make Annie's parents think all was well and that she actually took a greater part in looking after the children and household duties.

Annie's Mother took one look at Simon and fell in love. She was horrified at the run down state of Annie. She told her to go upstairs and pack her bag as she was going to go home with them. Mrs Gates started to say that this wasn't possible, she would have to give proper notice, etc. Annie's father told her that as Annie received no wages she was in fact a volunteer and she was withdrawing her labour. If Mrs Gate made anymore fuss, he would notify the authorities of the conditions and hours that she had been forced to work, and reminded Mrs Gates that Annie was only 18.

Philip had travelled up with Annie's parents but had stayed outside as he felt so angry at the Gates that it was decided that it would be better for her parents to sort the situation out.

So Simon and Annie returned home. The neighbours surprised Annie's Mum and were very supportive and not judgmental in the least. Philip's parents also soon fell in love with Simon.

Three months later the couple were allowed to get married, and 30 years later and with three more offspring they were still together.

Annie never forgot her friends in the house and had been delighted to hear from Norma that her baby had been returned to her. Christmas cards and birthday cards were sent every year. She prayed for Molly and Margot but did not communicate with them in case it brought back bad memories.

Chapter 28

The cases against Agnes Dayton and Alice Green had never been concluded. The papers that had been taken from the house showed that money had been taken from prospective adoptive parents for several years.

These parents had been carefully selected by Alice Green. The criteria for the particular couples being selected were; the couple wished the adoption to be secret. Many couples found it hard to admit that they were unable to have their own children and they would go through a fake pregnancy prior to receiving their adopted baby. There were other reasons for an adoption to be kept secret and the investigating officers were amazed at some of the excuses they were given when the adoptive parents were interviewed.

The welfare department checked the children in the cases that were uncovered and found they were all in very good homes and very much loved.

It did not appear that any other child had been in the situation of Norma's little boy. The reason for the extra-large payment demanded from the Abdullah's was, they wanted a child of mixed race and in the sixties this was harder to find. Mr Abdullah belonged to minor royalty in the Arab world, an adopted son and heir would not have been accepted by his family.

None of the parents wanted to pursue Dayton or Green in the courts, even if it had been possible. They were more frightened that a court may have tried to remove their beloved children.

The files on Dayton and Green were filed away and would only be looked at if Dayton or Green tried to re-enter the UK and it was likely that one or both of them could now be dead.

Sharon's life since the adoption of her son had changed. She had returned to the bosom of her family and all the material assets…but the wild child had gone. She no longer wanted to go clubbing or to parties. In fact, when her parents gave a dinner party it was an effort to get Sharon to put in an appearance.

Her parents put this metamorphosis down to maturity and were not really interested enough to talk to her about her feelings.

On her child's first birthday, Sharon had taken an overdose and the hospital were lucky to save her. Her parents had been mortified, more because of the embarrassment her suicide attempt had caused than any other reason. Her father paid for her to go into a private clinic and had thought that would 'sort the girl out' as he had put it.

While Sharon was in the clinic she met the senior consultant there, Rupert Fleming. He was 15 years older and a widower, but this was of no concern to Sharon. She liked his company and he fell head over heels in love with her. Six months after she had left the clinic Rupert asked Sharon to marry him.

Sharon wasn't in love with Rupert, although she had become fond of him. Her capacity for deep emotional attachment seemed to be buried deep inside, which she accepted. So she agreed to marry Rupert. She had made it very clear to him that she did not want any children. This was not a major concern to Rupert as he had a son from his first marriage.

Sharon had settled into a quiet kind of life. Rupert liked walking and he had bought Sharon two Labrador puppies soon after their marriage and the dogs became her focus as had other dogs through the years.

Her parents had forbidden her to tell Rupert about her past. Even while she was in the clinic they had concocted the story that her depression had been caused by the loss of her pony.

Thirty years later she had kept her secret. She was happily childless, she told her friends. Inside her head she still had her son; she talked to him in her mind sometimes. He was her secret and a secret she hugged closely. No-one else could share him, because to share him would mean someone would try and take his memory away.

Chapter 29

Margot had thought long and hard over her husband's suggestion of trying to find Sonny. One day she was all for it, then the next all the clouds of doubt would descend.

Peter had taken his friend John into his confidence. He had known John since they had been to school together and Peter knew that it had been safe to tell John about Sonny.

John understood the turmoil that mothers of adopted children went through. He knew there was always that deep longing to find the lost child but there was always the fear of rejection and the feelings of failure because they had abandoned their babies.

Peter did not discuss the matter any further with Margot, but he knew she was still mulling it over in her mind.

One morning while they were having breakfast, Peter told his wife that he had to go to Leeds the following week to see the bishop. There was a meeting of the clergy to discuss changes that the church was considering.

"The meeting will last about three hours and I wondered if you would like to come with me, darling? Perhaps you could go and see your friend Norma while I am at the meeting. Then we could have a meal on our way home."

Margot thought for a minute. She had not been back to Leeds since Sonny's adoption.

"Yes I think it's time I put the past behind me. I would love to see Norma again if she is willing to meet. I will write to her to see if it is possible to go for a visit, and will give her our phone number to ring to arrange it if she is happy about it.

Peter was delighted. He felt this would be a move forward and perhaps let her reconsider trying to find Sonny.

So Margot sat down and wrote a letter to Norma. Within a couple of days, Norma was on the phone, absolutely thrilled at the prospect of seeing her friend Margot again.

Norma knew that it was due to Margot and Annie that she had got her son back. She had often been tempted to write to Margot and invite her to visit, but had been afraid that it would upset Margot too much to go back into the past.

The weather was sunny on the day of the visit to Leeds. Peter went off to his meeting and Margot had a wander through the town towards the market. Being there again didn't bring back too many memories as many things had changed, but the market still seemed to be nearly the same.

Margot had bought a beautiful azalea plant from her own garden that she had grown, as a gift for Norma and her aunt. She knew that Norma had got married to a lad from the market, she had been told it was Big Mick's son, by the Christmas cards Norma had sent, she had said she was so happy, and Barry her husband adored Billy her son.

As she reached what used to be Linda's market stall, she saw a young man in charge. Margot approached uncertainly.

"Excuse me," she said hesitantly, "I am looking for Linda and Norma."

The man came from behind the stall said, "You must be Margot, we are so glad you wanted to come, it has been her one wish to see you again."

"You must be Barry. I am very happy to come to see Norma."

Barry took her hand.

"Please don't take this the wrong way but if it is possible, it would make Norma so happy to have you back in her life, not just for a flying visit. If it hadn't been for you and your friend, we wouldn't have got our Billy back."

As Margot had never been to the Spicer's home, Barry had to give her directions. It was only a street away from the market.

116

As Margot turned into the street, she saw Norma sitting on the wall outside one of the cottages. She leapt up and ran to greet Margot. Both women were in tears. It was clear that the intervening years had been good to them both.

Norma was still slight, but now she was a mature young woman. Her hair was shoulder length and her eyes sparkled. Not the downtrodden child that Margot remembered. No bitten nails, but nicely manicured and painted a subtle pink.

Norma was delighted to see the change in her friend also. Margot was now on the chubby side. Her hair had lightened over the years and was cut in a stylish bob.

The two women went into the house to be greeted by Linda, who hugged Margot with great gusto. Henry, who suffered with arthritis, was sitting in his chair. "Eh, lass, it's good to see you, where's this husband of yours?"

"I gave him your address and he will call later to pick me up. I made him drop me in town as I wanted to have a wander, but it all seems so different now," Margot replied.

Margot looked around and saw lots of photos. Norma saw her looking.

"Yes, that is our Bill. William Henry Spicer Brown as he insists on being called. Linda and Henry were allowed to officially adopt me. The court looked for my birth mother, but they found that she had died from a drug overdose when I was 15, so there was no problem about me being adopted."

The photos showed a handsome boy; from his school photos to one wearing a mortarboard and gown.

"He went to university and studied law," Norma proudly told Margot.

"He is now a junior in a law firm in Leeds, we are so proud of him."

"Who are the two little girls?"

Norma looked at her mother.

Linda took Margot's hand, "They are Billy's sisters, we haven't told you as we were afraid of upsetting you."

Margot understood and said, "That is wonderful, please don't worry, I am so pleased you have your little family. Peter and I have not been blessed with children of our own; perhaps we can be aunty and uncle to yours. What are their names?"

Norma was relieved, "They are twins, Margaret Rose, and Anna Linda. I wanted to remember my two friends who gave me back my life and my son!"

Margot was so touched that she burst into tears.

The day went too quickly. Linda and Henry went out into the garden to see Barry plant the Azalea. Henry supervised the event.

"I will be able to sit by my lovely plant and think of you now," Norma said.

Peter arrived at about four in the afternoon and was invited to stay for a wonderful tea that Linda and Norma had prepared.

Henry took Peter to one side, "That lass of yours is a diamond, we all owe her so much. I wish there was some way we could repay her."

Peter found himself confiding in Henry about his plan to try and find Sonny Jim.

"If I can do anything to help, lad, I still have contacts in the police, just let me know. That girl deserves to find her son, but as you say it can be a sticky road and sometimes these things don't always go well."

The girls sat out in the garden and Margot told Norma and Linda all about her life with Peter. They were so pleased that she was so happy, neither mentioned Sonny but he was there in all their minds.

Eventually, Margot told her friends that Peter had suggested trying to find Sonny. She told them that she wasn't sure it was fair to intrude on Sonny's life.

"Perhaps Sonny would like to find his mother," Linda said. "It may be worth letting Peter make some enquiries, love."

"Has Billy ever asked about his father?" Margot asked.

"When he was 21, he asked me to tell him. I told him the truth. He took it very well and in a way it bound us closer together. We have known Barry and his father for years and when Barry asked me to marry him, Billy was delighted. Ever since we have been married he has called Barry, Dad."

Norma then told Margot her story.

"I was taken away from my birth mother when I was very small. I lived in various foster homes till I was 14.

I came over funny at school one day; my form teacher took me to the sick bay.

My temperature was normal, and the nurse started asking me about my menstrual cycle. I had no idea what she was talking about. Then she asked me if I had let a boy do things to me. I got scared and cried.

She went off and came back with the head mistress.

I was so scared, Miss French, the head mistress, told my form mistress to leave us. She was very nice to me, gave me a cup of tea.

So I told her what had happened.

The foster mother I was living with worked in a bakery. She had brought some cakes home and told me to take some over onto the estate for her mother. I hated going onto the estate where her mother lived.

When I moaned, my foster mother called me a selfish little cow. All she was worried about was getting down the pub with the bloke she was knocking about with.

So it was easier to do as I was asked, so I took the cakes over to the old lady, who actually was quite a nice old dear. On the way back, I had gone across the grass between the blocks of flats instead of keeping to the well-lit paths. I just wanted to get home quickly.

I had seen a group of boys standing by the doorway of the next block of flats. I hurried past but then realized they were following me. They caught up with me and pulled me round the side of the block. My duffle coat was pulled off and my trousers and knickers. I kicked and yelled, they told me to shut up or they would kill me.

I shut my eyes and what happened next was hard for me to explain to my head teacher. What they did hurt me, then they ran off laughing. I picked my clothes up and got dressed and ran home. My foster mother had gone down the pub so I washed myself and went to bed.

So when I had explained all this, the welfare lady came and after a doctor had examined me I was carted off to the house where I met you."

"Oh, Norma, how awful!" Margot was horrified.

"No, please don't feel sad, not now. Look at what I have got. A proper Mum and Dad, a wonderful husband and three beautiful children."

Very soon it was time for Peter and Margot to leave. Margot had re-found her friend and knew they would be friends for the rest of her life and promised to keep in touch. She had asked Norma and her family to visit her and Peter.

On the way home, Margot was thoughtful.

"I think I would like to try and find Sonny Jim, Peter."

"I will speak to John Hannay to see what he advises as how we go about it."

Peter was relieved as now he could proceed with Margot's blessing.

Even as Margot had said those words she knew that it was the right thing to do. If she didn't find Sonny, she still had her memories of the beautiful child she had so briefly held in her arms and no one could ever take those memories away.

Chapter 30

At the museum, Emily Johnson was an enthusiastic worker. Molly was pleased she had chosen her for the job. Emily was spellbound by the exhibits and artefacts and Molly knew she went to the library to find books to learn more on the history of some of the pieces in the cabinets.

Molly decided she would put her name forward as a candidate for a curator's course. Molly had enjoyed the course many years ago and it had made it possible for her to obtain the position she now held.

Emily was thrilled when Molly asked her if this was something she would like to do. The course didn't start until the following September which gave Molly time to put forward her recommendation for Emily to receive funds to go on the course.

This was approved and Emily was delighted.

Several of the displays on show were of iron-age weaponry and in one cabinet was a reconstructed skull thought to be of an Iron Age man. They jokingly called him Fred! As you walked around the museum, Fred's glass eyes seemed to follow you.

One day as Emily was polishing the glass cabinet where Fred was displayed she said, "I suppose if skulls of our ancestors were dug up we could find out what they looked like."

"Might not be a good idea," said Molly laughing, "especially if they were ugly!"

"I don't know what my real parents looked like, as I was adopted as a baby," Emily said looking sad.

Molly felt sad for the girl but the phone rang just as Emily had spoken and Molly went back to her desk.

Although no more was said on the subject that day, as Molly lay in bed that night she couldn't get Emily's sad face out of her mind. They were exceedingly busy over the next few days as several schools had booked in for tours. Molly had trained Emily to do some of the tours and she seemed to enjoy taking the children round the museum and answering their questions.

The following week Molly was upstairs in the admin office checking on the time of the next school booking.

"Can I see the staff application files for a minute Janet?" Molly asked.

She took them back down the stairs to her desk. Emily had taken the afternoon off as she had a dental appointment.

Molly found Emily's application form which the now retired Hilary had neatly filed along with the other staff members. All the job applications had always gone straight to admin and Hilary had weeded out the applicants and given Molly the list of the candidates that she thought worthy of an interview. Hilary had given a short review of past employment history, education and the age of each applicant. She had been doing the job for so long that Molly knew she was getting the best applicants and it saved her a lot of time.

Now looking at Emily's file, she almost felt she was prying. But something made her continue.

Emily's date of birth was the same as Dinah's.

This took Molly's breath away for a minute.

"No don't be so silly, there are a lot of children born every day!" she told herself.

Molly still pondered over Emily and decided to try and get to know her a little better.

The next day Molly asked Emily if she would like to go for a fish and chip supper after work.

"I would love to, but I have to go and visit my mother who is in a nursing home. I have to catch the five o'clock bus out to Mettering where the home is. There isn't a later bus, perhaps we could do it another night. They only let you visit in the evenings from six to seven and they won't let visitors in until right on the dot of six."

"Mettering is only a 20 minute bus ride, so you have to hang about till six then?" Molly enquired.

"Yes. Mother doesn't always know me, I promised Dad that I would go every week to see her. He died last year and he made me promise."

"We close the museum at four, so why don't we go and get our fish and chips and then I will drive you over to Mettering. It looks like rain and I'm not in a hurry to get home. My dreadful neighbour has trimmed the hedge between my house and his and he is going to clear up the mess he made tonight. So I wanted to be out as he is very hard to get rid of once he starts talking, plus he starts hinting about me making him tea."

Emily laughed, she had seen the 'dreadful neighbour' once when she had dropped into Molly's with a birthday card that she had forgotten to take to work to give Molly.

"Well if you don't mind that would be lovely. I smelt the fish and chips as I went over to post the letters and my mouth started to water."

So that evening they sat and ate their supper together in the little chip shop across the road from the museum. Molly wanted to ask so many questions, but was too nervous.

Molly had bought a pot of tea for them both and nearly put milk into Emily's cup.

"Oops, nearly forgot, you don't take milk do you."

Emily was intolerant to some dairy products, cow's milk being her main problem.

Emily was the one who started to tell Molly about her adoptive mother and father. The more Emily told her the more Molly began to believe that Emily could possibly be her Dinah.

"My father was a heart specialist," she said. "But he died of a heart attack, how awful was that? My mother had been diagnosed with dementia two years previously, we struggled to look after her. So my Dad found the Home for her through his medical pals. It is expensive, but we both wanted the best for and she is looked after very well. I don't think she even knows that Dad has died. He left a large trust for her so the fees are covered."

"How sad for you both."

Molly wanted ask a lot more questions but didn't as there were too many thoughts whizzing around in her head.

Florrie had told her that Dinah's adoptive father was a heart specialist. It was information that Molly should not have been told. But Florrie knew she would worry about the heart condition that they had detected in Dinah.

Coincidence probably, thought Molly.

The evening went well. Molly was tempted to accompany Emily into the home as she was invited, but Molly said she would sit in the car and read her newspaper.

It would have been nice to see the woman who just may have been the mother who had cared for Dinah all these years. Molly put all these thoughts out of her mind and studied her paper.

On the way home, Molly decide to broach the subject again.

"How did you find out you were adopted?"

"My mother told me when I was six. She thought she couldn't have children of her own but when I was five she had a baby boy. But they didn't treat me any different to Martin, my brother. But I think she told me because we were so different in looks. Martin was blond, blue eyed and I have always been darker and brown eyed. Martin lives in America now."

"Have you ever wondered about your birth mother, Emily?"

Just at that point, they got back into the traffic and Molly changed the subject into the 'wretched road hogs' and laughed at some drunk tottering across the road in front of them. Suddenly Molly didn't want to know.

Emily didn't reply to the question and Molly was afraid of the answer she might receive.

Molly dropped Emily off at her home and made her way very thoughtfully back to her house.

When she got indoors, the light was flashing on her phone telling her that she had a message. She switched the answer phone on and was surprised to hear a message from Jane. She sounded a bit upset and was asking Molly to give her a call back. Although they had exchanged telephone numbers years ago, neither had ever talked on the phone. Molly, because she was afraid that James could pick up the phone and Jane because she felt awkward because Molly had lost Dinah.

So after she had taken her coat off, Molly returned Jane's call.

"Hi, Jane, long time no hear, are you all right, you sounded a bit upset?"

Jane was so pleased to hear her friend, she felt like bursting into tears.

"I was hoping we could have a meet up soon. I feel it's time. We have just come back from a holiday in Spain, Jonathon and his family came too."

"Oh that was nice for you."

"It should have been and it was lovely to see the grandchildren, but James was his usual infuriating self. Chatting up everything in a skirt. Even Jonathon noticed and had to tell his father to behave a couple of times.

I have really had enough of his behaviour Molly. When we got back, there were messages on the phone from some female from his work, very inappropriate messages! Please can we meet, you are the only person who knows what he is capable of?"

Yes she knew what James was capable of, but had hoped the years would have tamed him a bit.

They agreed to meet at a pub about halfway between their two homes for lunch the following Saturday.

When Jane put the phone down, she felt a modicum of relief. She heard James outside the front door talking on his phone, so in passing the door she opened it and he quickly closed his phone.

"What you doing creeping about, you're like creeping Jesus!"

"I was just going to ask you what you wanted for your dinner and normal people don't stand outside talking on their phone unless they have something to hide."

Jane left him standing there and returned to the kitchen.

To hell with him, she thought. She went up to run herself a bath.

By the following Saturday, Jane had decide she wanted out. She had the money that her mother had left her plus the money from the sale of her parents' house. James had tried many times to get her to invest in one of his mad schemes. The fact that she refused had been a bone of contention between them for the past three years since she had inherited the money. Her mother had been wise enough to put the money in a trust fund, as she had never trusted James.

Molly had put all thoughts of Dinah out of her mind for the time being. She more worried about Jane. She knew only too well what a manipulator James could be.

The two women met as planned. Of the two Molly seemed to have fared the best. Jane looked a downtrodden exhausted woman. She had lost weight in the past year and her clothes hung on her. Molly could see what the strain caused by James was doing to her friend.

Molly told Jane that she was welcome to move in with her until the situation could be sorted out. Jane didn't want to burden her son with her problems so Molly's kind offer was possibly one that Jane would be consider. She had some serious thinking to do and wanted to consult her solicitor.

Jane felt so much better for sharing her problems with Molly and went home very determined to make a better life for herself.

It was Jane's birthday the following weekend and Jonathon and his family were coming up on the Friday evening. Jane had decided that it would be an opportunity to tell her son her decision. She knew James would go for his Saturday morning round of golf regardless that his son was visiting; nothing got in the way of his golf!

Jane cooked a lovely meal on the Friday afternoon ready for the family when they arrived. James went to the station to pick Jonathon and family up and by six o'clock they were all sitting enjoying the meal. James as usual, was over halfway through his bottle of red wine before they had finished their first course. Jane disliked red wine and her and Jonathon had a glass of white wine. Jonathon's wife Laura did not drink.

James went to fill his glass and spilt a puddle of wine onto the beautiful white tablecloth. Jane got up to get a cloth to mop up the spillage when James bellowed at her,

"Don't make such a fuss, woman, sit down and get on with your dinner."

Jonathon looked at his father in disgust.

"Dad there is no need to shout at Mum, it's a lovely tablecloth and will stain if it's not mopped up!"

James stood up and leered at his son, swaying a little, "Still a sissy boy, then I suppose you will go and wash it out for your stupid Mumsy Wumsy!"

Jonathon went to stand up, but Laura put her hand on his arm.

With that James picked up the bottle and staggered out the door. They heard the front door slam and a car start up.

"My God, he's not driving in that state is he?" Jonathon ran to the front door in time to see his father's car drive out of the driveway.

Laura went and put her arms around her mother in law.

"We knew he was becoming a nightmare. We saw what he was like when we were in Spain. How long has he been like this?"

Jane wiped her tears and told her family what she intended to do.

"The house will have to be sold of course. I am going to stay with my friend Molly after I have spoken to my solicitor."

Jane loved her home; she had put her heart into the furnishings and the garden. Jonathon knew it would be hard for her to lose it.

"Why should you move out, Mum, it's him that is being unreasonable."

"Look lets enjoy your visit, I have been looking forward to seeing you. I am glad the children had an early dinner and were in bed and didn't witness their grandfather's behaviour. He will probably go to the golf club and get a taxi home. We will all be in bed by that time and tomorrow he may be in a better mood. I will deal with things after the weekend and probably go down to stay with Molly while the solicitor is sorting things out."

After the dishes were stacked away, they played a few games of cards. At around nine o'clock, Jane got up to make some hot chocolate as she knew Laura enjoyed this. Jonathon preferred another glass of white wine with his mother.

As they sat talking, the front doorbell rang.

"I'll go, Mum, perhaps it's Dad can't find his keys!"

The women heard voices; then Jonathon came back into the lounge accompanied by a police officer and a policewoman.

"Mum, there has been an accident. It's Dad."

"I am sorry, Mrs Robertson, your husband's car went off the road into a tree. We think he must have died instantly. Had he been drinking?"

The rest of the evening became a blur to Jane. Their doctor was called and Jane was given something to help her sleep. Jonathon went to the hospital to identify his father, while Laura stayed with Jane.

Jonathon and Laura stayed for the following week and took care of all the funeral arrangements.

Jane felt numb but also a little guilty. Friends called to commiserate at her loss.

"I feel nothing, Laura, the man I married no longer existed. It was as if he had left years ago, in fact I am not sure if he really was the man I thought he was. All I was left with was this arrogant argumentative man!"

Laura felt she understood as ever since she had met James she had wondered what Jane had seen in him and she prayed that Jonathon would not turn out like his father.

A week after the funeral Molly phoned Jane. She was concerned because she hadn't heard anything from Jane, so she plucked up courage and phoned her. She had decided if James answered the phone she would just hang up. Her number was not listed so she knew James could not call her back. But Jane answered her call.

When Jane told Molly the news, she was shocked and immediately offered to go over to see Jane. Jonathon and family had now gone back to London so Jane was pleased that her friend had offered to visit. They arranged that Molly would drive up at the weekend and stay for a few days. Molly hadn't taken any holiday so she was able to be absent from the museum. She knew her staff could cope very well without her.

Molly had not asked Emily anymore about her family or her adoption. She was scared to probe further. Molly also felt that Emily had enough problems with her poor sick mother. So a few days away with Jane would be good for her.

Molly drove over on the Saturday morning to Jane's address. When she saw Jane's beautiful house and garden, she was very impressed. It was obvious that a lot of love had been put into the garden by Jane and her taste inside the house was excellent.

Molly felt sorry about James's death and understood how Jane felt about it. Apparently Jonathon wasn't deeply grieving for his father either. James had persistently verbally abused his son for years all because Jonathon had no interest in playing golf or going on drinking binges with his father.

Jane was afraid to bring up the subject of the 'house in Leeds' as she didn't want to bring back bad memories for Molly. She was surprised when Molly brought up the subject.

"I had a wonderful letter from Margot; she went back to Leeds to visit Norma."

Jane knew all about Norma's story as she had regularly received updates from Margot, but she hadn't heard about the visit to Leeds.

"Margot told me that her and Peter had a lovely day with Norma and her family. Apparently Norma has also got twin girls. She hadn't told any of us as she was afraid of upsetting me and Margot, her being so happy and us losing our babes."

"Oh bless her, but I know Margot would have been so happy for her."

"They are going to keep in closer touch and Norma, Barry and the children are going over to stay for a weekend very soon."

It gave the two women something pleasant to think about.

Jane told Molly that now she wouldn't have to sell her much loved house. Jonathon had suggested that he and his family sold their house in London and moved back up to Yorkshire. Jonathon could relocate in his job easily.

Jane had been delighted at the suggestion. They were now thinking of building a granny annex onto Jane's house as she no longer needed such a large house. This way she would still have her beloved garden and see her family every day.

"It is nice that Margot keeps in contact with us. She still really misses Sonny Jim. She is so happy with her vicar, but I know she still thinks of her boy."

"I know I was the lucky one, I still have my son, but we never forget the lost ones do we?" Jane took Molly's hand as she spoke.

That evening they sat on the patio having a coffee, watching the sun go down. The sky was turning the wonderful colours that no painter can reproduce. A blackbird was singing his evening song as the day slipped away. The perfumes from Jane's garden were soporific.

Molly said quietly, "I think I could have found Dinah!"

Molly was astonished that she had spoken out loud. Jane looked at Molly.

"What did you say?" She asked.

"Oh ignore me, I um…"

Jane took Molly's hand, "You think you have found Dinah? Can you tell me?"

Molly knew that Jane was the only person in the world she could share her suspicions with. So she told her about Emily.

"But just because she is adopted and her birthday is the same as Dinah's doesn't make her my daughter. But she did tell me that her father, who is now dead, was a heart surgeon. But it could all be coincidence!"

Molly got up and took their coffee cups back into the kitchen. Jane didn't pursue the conversation any further. She knew that Molly would tell her more when she was ready. It was all too tender a subject to try and dissect any more at the moment.

Molly returned home the next morning. Feeling relieved that she had shared her thoughts a little with Jane. But she wasn't ready to dig deeper at the moment.

Chapter 31

Sharon was still content with her life with Rupert. She had come out her shell a little more and was happy to give the odd dinner party for Rupert's colleagues and their friends. They had a beautiful home which gave Sharon a lot of pleasure. She liked shopping and had acquired good taste.

She didn't mix much with female friends only occasionally going to a spar with them for a relaxing day now and then.

One morning in the late autumn, a letter came for Sharon. She rarely received letters and this one looked quite official.

"What's this, another beauty treatment clinic touting for custom?" Rupert said as he passed the letter to her.

"I expect so, I'll have a look after breakfast. It's usually someone trying to sell some outrageously priced beauty preparation. Jasmine gives out all her friends' addresses hoping to get free samples for herself."

She put the letter on the sideboard and actually forgot about it until later that afternoon.

She noticed the letter as she was going up to have a bath, so she took it with her. She put it on her bed and went and turned the taps on for her bath.

She started to open the letter, and then the phone rang so she laid it on the bed.

It was her friend, Felicity, so excited because her husband had just been elected as captain at the golf club and she had to tell someone!

Felicity had to boast about every facet of her life. Sharon was not over keen on her but because Rupert and her husband were friends Sharon felt she had to tolerate her. They talked for a few minutes then Sharon remembered that her bath water was running and terminated the conversation.

Sharon undressed and slipped into her bath. She liked the water hot and full of perfumed bubbles. It was one of her guilty pleasures. She lay there till she heard Rupert's car pull up in their drive. The front door opened and Rupert called out to see where she was.

He came into their bedroom and started to remove his business suit. Sharon reluctantly got out of her warm bubbly cocoon and put her dressing gown on.

"What's this, darling?" Rupert had picked up Sharon's letter.

"I don't know as I was opening it Felicity rang, crowing about her husband being made captain of the golf club!"

"Ha ha, he only got voted in because no-one else wanted the job," Rupert said laughing.

He looked at the letter then thrust it at Sharon.

"I hope this is a joke, or perhaps they have got the wrong Sharon Peterson! Or perhaps some rich uncle has died and left you a fortune."

Sharon took the letter. When she read the letter heading, her knees went weak, she sat down on the bed.

FIND YOUR PAST

Dear Mrs Fleming

We are seeking a lady by the name of Sharon Peterson.

Our research shows that this was your maiden name.

The person we are looking for was staying in Leeds at an address in Russett Avenue in1961.

If any of the above details refer to you, we would be happy to hear from you.

We will give further details of the nature of our enquiry on receiving proof of your identity and a copy of your birth certificate.

Yours

Sharon threw the letter onto the bed.

"I have never been to Leeds, it's a dump or so I have heard."

Inside she was shaking, but bravado came to the rescue.

She picked the letter up and threw it in the bin,

"Not me, I am afraid, now let me get dressed."

They both changed into casual clothes as some friends were coming round for the evening…

"No need for fancy stuff tonight, old girl, it's just Wally and Mary, they usually come dressed as though they have been in the garden all day!"

Rupert had already forgotten the letter. He enjoyed these particular friends company more than any other and the evening usually ended up as a card school. Sharon's daily help had prepared some cold dishes for supper so all she had to do was get them from the fridge and put some plates and knives and forks on the table. They like to help themselves on these very informal evenings.

Inside Sharon had butterflies.

Later after their guests had gone, Rupert brought the subject of the letter up again.

"I hope you haven't got some hidden past that is going to leap out of the wardrobe at us, darling!"

Sharon tried to laugh,

"I am not sure my father would be too pleased to hear you accusing me of a disreputable past. Remember he has promised to donate a large cheque to your research programme darling!"

Rupert thought that he had better drop the subject as Sharon's fathers promised donation was an integral part of the future of the mental health programme he was trying to set up, and he wasn't known for his sense of humour especially where his family's reputation was concerned.

Sharon went up to bed before Rupert. She retrieved the screwed up letter from the bin and hid it in the bottom of her handbag.

Nothing more was said about the letter. Sharon put it out of her mind although she did hide the letter in her jewellery safe!

Chapter 32

Molly returned from her visit still feeling sad for Jane.

James had been so unkind and had obviously made his family's life unhappy for quite a while.

She was not sure she should have told Jane about Emily. But it was done now and Jane had not questioned her as to what she was going to do about it. Molly herself didn't know the answer to that either.

Her first day back at the museum and all seemed to have run all right in her absence, but Emily wasn't there.

Molly asked Frank and David if they knew why Emily had not arrived to work. Neither of them had any idea. They said she had been OK, the day before.

Molly rang Emily's number a few times but didn't get any reply. So by five o'clock Molly was really concerned. Molly decided she would drive over to the little house where Emily lived.

Her father had bought her the house as an investment. Initially the house had been rented out and Emily had lived at home with her father. When her father died, her brother and Emily had decided to sell the large family home and add the proceeds to the trust that paid for their mother's nursing home. Emily had moved into her little terrace house, which she loved.

Molly parked her car and walked up to the front door of Emily's house and rang the bell. She saw a shadow through the frosted glass in the door.

"It's me, Emily. I was worried about you."

The door opened a very bedraggled Emily opened the door.

"Come in, it was nice of you to come."

Emily led the way through the hallway into a small lounge. The smell of lavender polish was strong and the room was prettily furnished.

"I will make some tea. I am sorry that I didn't phone. I have been at the hospital all day. My mother had a stroke in the night; I have been sitting with her all day."

A tear ran down Emily's cheek.

"She died at four o'clock this afternoon."

Molly went over to Emily and took her into her arms. Emily just melted into Molly's arms and wept.

At that moment, Molly knew that this girl was her Dinah. The smell of her skin, the complete feeling of closeness. The maternal instinct? She could never describe the feelings she felt as she comforted the distraught girl.

Common sense took over as she sat Emily down.

"I will make us a cup of tea, then you can go up and pack a bag and you are coming back home with me for the night."

Molly made some tea and after they had drunk it Emily seemed to be a lot calmer.

"I phoned my brother from the hospital and he is coming over in a couple of days' time. The almoner at the hospital contacted the funeral directors and we just have to decide the format of the funeral, which I will do when Martin gets here."

Molly drove Emily back to her home, and cooked some tea for them both. Emily was now able to talk of her mother now.

"Mother was never good at coping with life. She relied a lot on my father. When she started forgetting things, we didn't notice at first, but it quickly got worse. We hated having to put her into a Home, but she would wander off in her nightclothes and needed 24 hour care."

"Well, she is now re-united with your dad, if that is what happens.

It's what we like to think anyway!" Molly said.

"She was never a 'cuddly' mother, in fact I don't remember her ever having either me or Martin on her lap! But she was my Mum."

Emily had another little weep.

Molly's old dog came over and licked Emily's hand, she wiped her tears away and sat on the floor with Bobby and they soon had a tug of war going on with the dog's toys.

Molly went upstairs and made sure the spare room was tidy. Very soon it was obvious that Emily needed to sleep, so Molly suggested she had a nice warm bath and then go to bed. Gratefully Emily climbed the stairs and was very soon sleeping.

Molly sat for an hour or so deep in thought. Emily had just lost the only mother she had ever known, so any thoughts Molly might have had had be put to one side. It was not necessary to burden the girl any more.

In Molly's mind, she was sure that Emily was Dinah; that should be enough. She had found her beautiful daughter. Molly decided that was all she could wish for.

To be acknowledged as the woman who had abandoned her was a frightening step. It could ruin the relationship she had with Emily.

Molly's mother used to say 'a little piece of cake is better than none'.

So Molly went to her bed her decision made.

Emily took the rest of the week off and her brother Martin came and stayed with her until their mother's funeral Molly went to the funeral, she felt that she owed Emily's mother a debt of gratitude for caring for Emily.

Chapter 33

Since receiving the letter, Sharon had thrown herself into a whirlwind of outings. Her husband was pleased to see his wife so occupied. Shopping trips to London, followed by theatre with Felicity. Which did surprise Rupert as he always thought Sharon was not too keen on Felicity's company.

She had a couple of days stay at a health spar with her cousin Lucinda. She seemed to have a full diary of outings planned.

All to keep her mind from thinking about the letter!

Rupert had to go to Switzerland to visit a clinic that was trying out some new procedures that he was keen to observe. He would be away for five days. When he returned, they had booked a cruise to the Med, which Sharon was actually looking forward to.

The day before Rupert returned, Sharon was in her bedroom packing her suitcase for her holiday. She took a chiffon scarf over to the window with a new blouse she had bought, to check if the colours matched. As she held up the clothes, something caught her eye in the garden. There was a man standing behind the large rhododendron bush at the edge of the lawn. He had a bright yellow polo shirt, which is what had caught her eye.

She drew back behind the curtain and watched.

George, their gardener came out of the gardening shed and walked towards the man. They had a conversation. George then walked towards the house.

Sharon went downstairs. George always had a cup of tea in the kitchen when he was working. Her daily help was not coming in today so Sharon was going to make George his tea and she was curious.

"Hello, George, who was that man in the garden?"

"Well, Missus, he seemed a bit confused. He asked if the lady of the house was called Sharon, and did I know if you were a Peterson afore you were wed."

"What did you tell him?"

"Well I said I didn't rightly know what your maiden name was. 'Course I did, but didn't think you would want me to discuss your business with a stranger. He then asked if I would ask you if he could come in to speak to you. He was a well-spoken young man. He told me that he was looking for his mother and you might be able to help him. He didn't look all that well."

Sharon went cold inside.

"I don't know anything about people's children George. I have never had any or wanted any come to that. So please ask him to go, I cannot help him! Please make sure he goes and tell him not to come back!"

Sharon made George's tea which he took back to the garden, then she went back upstairs. She didn't look out of the bedroom window as she didn't want to see the man again.

She felt very shaken and was thankful that Rupert was not at home.

Rupert returned that evening a little earlier than Sharon had expected him. "Can we get away early in the morning, darling?" she asked.

"Perhaps we could have some breakfast on the way, I know you love those huge motorway breakfasts." Sharon wanted to get away from the house as soon as possible.

Rupert was happy to oblige as he did love the rare treat of a cholesterol breakfast as he called it.

Suitcases in car, and Sharon and Rupert were on the road to Southampton by seven o'clock next morning.

Chapter 34

Molly still enjoyed her work at the museum. Emily was taking the Curators Course and was really enjoying it.

There would come a time when Molly would want to retire and she hoped that she would be able to put Emily forward as her replacement.

Lately Emily had seemed a lot more relaxed. After the death of her mother she had seemed very restless. She had joined an art club and a local history club that she went to in the evenings. So with her studies for the curator's course her spare time was fairly full.

Occasionally Emily and Molly had supper together. Usually fish and chips in the café near the museum. Molly got great comfort from these couple of hours together.

One evening, Jane phoned Molly.

"Hi, Molly, this may sound an odd question, but has Emily joined an art club recently?

"Yes, why do you ask? She joined one a couple of months after her mother died."

"Jonathon has always been good at art, so we encouraged him to join a club. Since he and his family moved up here he has been so busy setting up this new office that we felt he should have some leisure time. So he joined Painters Pallette Art Club."

"Oh that is the one that Emily belongs to. Has something happened?"

"Actually I am not sure. Jonathon has been going to the club for four weeks now. Laura went to meet him a couple of weeks ago and found him in the pub next to the art club. She told me that he was with a dark haired female. When he saw Laura, he left the woman and told Laura she was one of the art group.

Then when Laura was washing the apron that Jonathon wears when he is painting, she found a telephone number on a piece of paper, with the message, 'call me soon'."

Molly didn't know what to say.

Jane continued, "Laura has always been afraid that Jonathon would turn out like his father, it had crossed my mind also."

"It may not have been Emily, there are other females in the class, so Emily told me."

"I spoke to Jonathon on the quiet, and questioned him. He said she was a new member and they just seemed to click in a friendly way! He got a bit hot under the collar with me so I let it drop."

"I will ask Emily if she has met any new friends at the club, as that was one of her reasons for joining, to make new friends. Jonathon and Laura always seemed so happy together."

Molly had visited several times when Jonathon and his family were staying, so she knew both him and Laura and their children.

The next day the two women were collating some new artefacts together when Molly broached the subject.

"How is the art club, have you met any new friends? Are there any young people there of your own age?"

Emily blushed and laughed, "Mostly wrinklies, but there are one or two younger people. Sorry, Molly, no offence meant!"

"Perhaps you will meet a nice young man there, it's about time you did!"

Emily smiled, "Maybe I will or perhaps I have."

The look on Emily's face worried Molly.

Later that night Molly phoned Jane.

"I have a bad feeling about this, Jane. Look can we meet? How about we meet at that pub on the Alcombe Road. I can get there for about five on Friday."

Jane was always pleased to meet Molly, so agreed as she felt that the situation was a bit worrying.

Molly knew that her secret regarding Dinah's father must now be shared with Jane. She was worried that it could damage her relationship with Jane, but if the two young people were getting close then action had to be taken.

A plan formed in Molly's head but Jane would have to agree.

Jane was already sitting in a window seat when Molly arrived on the Friday…

They ordered a cream tea each and while waiting for their food to arrive Molly took a deep breath and started talking.

"I am hoping that you will understand why I haven't told you this before, Jane.

When I got to the Registry office on the day of your wedding, I had a terrible shock. Your James was my Jim, Dinah's father!"

Jane took a moment to digest what her friend had just said.

Molly ploughed on quickly before her nerve failed her.

"Jim used to come to our office for the stationary order and we had a short affair. He told me he was single. I found out that I was pregnant after he ended the affair. I never told him I was pregnant.

So to see him again at the registry office and that he was Jonathon's father was a great shock. As he was going to marry you, I could not destroy any chance of happiness you could have."

"Oh, Molly, how awful you must have felt. Did James recognize you?"

"Yes, he came over and asked me if I was going to tell you of our affair. Of course I told him 'no'!"

"I wasn't in love with him, just flattered at the attention, and when he finished the affair I saw what a shallow person

143

he really was. So you see why there can be nothing between Jonathon and Emily.

Plus, possibly Emily may not be aware that he has a family."

Jane sat and thought what a terrible day Molly must have had on her wedding day. What a friend she had been.

"I have an idea," said Molly. "How about we arrange a meal together, I will bring Emily. We won't say that we know that they have already met, we play dumb! We will introduce Jonathon's wife and children to Emily. The reaction of Jonathon and Emily will be interesting.

If there is anything going on then we will have to prove Emily's parentage. There must be an original birth certificate somewhere from when I registered her birth in Leeds and an adoption certificate somewhere also. Plus there is always a DNA test, which, if my suspicions are right, then we will have to tell them that they are half siblings. That fact could be why they are attracted to each other."

"Ok, that sounds a good plan."

Jane had a lot of thinking to do on her way home. She couldn't be angry with Molly, but angry with James for deceiving them both as he must have been seeing both of them at the same time as Jonathon and Dinah were born within a week or so.

Molly asked Janet in her admin department to ask Emily for a copy of her birth certificate. She told her to tell her it was required to put in her records.

Emily brought it in the next morning.

Molly made a few phone calls pretending to be Emily. She requested a copy of Emily's original birth certificate prior to her adoption. Fortunately Molly must have got hold of the office junior in the registrar's office, as without too much hassle, and an extra payment for a quick delivery the certificate was purchased. Even Molly was surprised at her success and was sure that the girl had breached quite a few privacy regulations to agree to send the certificate.

Think she just wanted to get rid of me, thought Molly.

Now she would be on tender hooks until she saw the document, which once and for all would confirm or otherwise that Emily was her Dinah.

Molly had not intended to intrude on Emily's privacy but if Jonathon and she were getting too close something had to be done. Hopefully once Emily met Laura and her children, she would realize that Jonathon was not free and knowing Emily, Molly hoped she wouldn't want to be responsible for breaking up his family.

On reflection, Molly wondered if now that her mother was dead, and effectively Emily was an orphan as far as she knew, if she would dare to tell Emily, if the birth certificate proved that Molly was her birth mother.

She decided that she would see how the evening meal went with Jane and her family before even opening the letter she was to receive from the registry office.

Molly told Emily of the proposed meal and asked her if she would come with her. She told her it was her friend's wedding anniversary, the first since her husband's death and she didn't want to be alone that night, which was actually true. This was also the reason Jane gave to Jonathon and Laura.

Molly made the excuse for inviting Emily was she hated driving in the dark and often missed her turning and would be grateful for her company.

Emily happily agreed.

They had a girlie talk about what to wear, then decided that as it was a Friday, Emily would stay at Molly's after driving home after the meal.

The restaurant was several miles away, but the reputation of the food was good.

Molly picked Emily up at six o'clock as arranged. Jane and Molly had agreed that Jane and family would get to the restaurant first and be seated by the time Molly and Emily arrived. They had decided that Jonathon and Laura should sit together beside Jane and Emily and Molly should sit opposite with the two children. That way Jane would have a good view of Emily's reaction on seeing Jonathon and Molly could see how Jonathon reacted.

Jane waved to Molly as they entered the restaurant.

"We have only just got here, come and sit down," Jane said.

"Hello, you must be Emily, sit there next to the monsters," she said, pointing to her grandchildren. This is Laura and Jonathon, my son and daughter in law and the monsters, their children!"

Emily smiled at Jane's grandchildren, shook hands with Laura, then laughing, she said, "Well hello Jonathon, I had no idea you were Molly's friend's son." She turned to Molly and said, "Jonathon goes to the same art club as me and we have had several chats."

Jonathon stood up and leant across the table and shook Emily's hand.

"This is nice and quite a coincidence. I was going to invite you to our place to meet Laura and the sprogs, as I think Laura was beginning to think I had another woman!"

Emily smiled and said, "Most of the members of the art club are, more mature than us. Did I say that right this time, Molly? So it was good that Jonathon was there. The others don't seem to have the same sense of humour as us do they?"

They settled down to order their meals and all chatted amicably together. Laura seemed to like Emily and they talked a lot about clothes they liked and shoes they would like to buy.

After the meal was over, Jane ordered coffee and asked Jonathon what he would like to drink. Emily said she would just like a mineral water.

"I have an intolerance to milk, so a mineral water would be fine."

Without thinking, Jane said, "So does Jonathon, he is like his father."

Molly poured the coffee for her and Jane realizing what she had said was afraid that her face would give her thoughts away. But no one else seemed to notice.

Both the women could see a likeness between Jonathon and Emily. They were amazed that Laura didn't see it.

The evening passed and everyone enjoyed the meal. They said their goodbyes and Molly and Emily took a slow drive home. Jonathon put two sleepy children into his car and drove his mother and family home.

"I liked Emily, she is lovely. We should invite her to come up with Molly when she comes to stay again," Laura said.

Jane's fears were abated for now.

The next, day Jane spoke to Molly on the phone.

"I think Emily is your Dinah, Molly. Did you see the resemblance? I was afraid Laura might say something!"

"I am waiting for the certificates from the registrar's office. I think then I will tell Emily my story about Dinah. I think I may tell her of my suspicions and be honest about how I got them to send me the certificates. I will then give her the unopened envelope and give her the choice of reading what is inside. What she chooses to do will be her decision. She may walk away, but it has to be her decision."

"Oh, Molly, Let's hope it will be alright. She couldn't have a more loving mother than you. If she is not Dinah, well we will face that then…"

Chapter 35

Sharon and Rupert returned from their cruise, both with lovely sun tans. They had wined and dined and danced the evenings away and investigated all the beautiful sights on the way.

Sharon seemed without a care in the world.

When they got home, as usual there was a large pile of post waiting for them. The daily help had prepared a meal for them and after they had eaten they settled down to open their mail.

Sharon nervously looked through her pile. She caught sight of the white envelope quickly and while Rupert was refilling his whisky glass she put it quickly into her pocket.

"I am just going up for a bath, darling," she said and went up to her bathroom.

She transferred the letter to her dressing gown pocket and hung it on the bathroom door. As she lay in her bath, she kept glancing at her dressing gown. While she had been away she had been thinking about the young man that had visited the house before they left for the cruise.

Her head was completely mixed up. She had come to no conclusions. One minute she thought, *what you don't know can't hurt you,* but doubts kept invading her head.

By the time she got out of the bath, she had made up her mind. She took the letter out of her pocket and stuffed it under the mattress on her bed. She then dressed herself and then went down stairs to join Rupert.

Chapter 36

A week after the meal they had shared with Jane and her family, it was Molly's birthday. The letter had arrived from the Registry Office and Molly had put it on the mantelpiece unopened. She had been sorely tempted to open it, but felt that it was Emily's place to do that as it was addressed to her.

Molly had asked Emily to come over and have a meal with her. Emily had wanted to take Molly out to a restaurant, but Molly had insisted she just wanted to cook a nice meal for them at home.

Emily turned up with a huge bunch of flowers and a bottle of Molly's favourite perfume.

Molly was a good cook and had cooked Emily's favourite, a lamb roast followed by a homemade sherry trifle.

After the meal, Molly said, "There is a beautiful sunset, let's go and watch the sun go down,"

They took their glasses of wine and sat on Molly's patio.

"There is something I would like to tell you. Whatever you feel after I have told you, I will respect."

Emily was a little frightened in case Molly was going to tell her that she was ill or something.

Molly took a deep breath, there was no going back now.

"Emily when I was in my early twenties I met a man. I had a brief affair, and after it was ended I found out that I was pregnant. I couldn't tell my mother, as she was very frail. In those days, for a girl to be pregnant out of marriage was considered a terrible thing. If I had told my mother, it could have killed her."

Emily took Molly's hand, "Oh, Molly, that is so sad!"

"I went to a mother and baby home in Leeds, from where the baby was adopted. It broke my heart in a million pieces, but I had no other choice."

Molly had to continue quickly as her nerve was fading fast.

"My little girl, had a heart defect, but was adopted. They told me that her adoptive father was a heart specialist."

Emily went to speak, but Molly held her hand up and quickly continued.

"I just thought it could be a coincidence when you told me that your father was a heart specialist but it made me wonder. I went and looked on your application form to see when your birthday was. Your date of birth was the same as my Dinah. Yes, my darling daughter was registered as Dinah. I couldn't say anything while your mother was alive, but it has kept eating away at me. It could all be just a coincidence, but I had to know.

"So I did something very bad, for which I apologise.

I contacted the Registrar's Office, pretending to be you and asked for a copy of your original birth certificate, using the details from the certificate that you gave Janet. I had to know, Emily, I loved my little girl so much and it all seemed too much of a coincidence. I am sorry, Emily."

Molly was exhausted with the emotion of her confession.

"Does that mean that you could be my natural mother?" Emily asked.

"I don't know. The letter came back from the Registrar's Office last week. It is not my letter to open; the letter is addressed to you. Now you can open it – or if you would rather destroy the letter unopened that is your decision. I am sorry for deceiving you, but I felt we should know the truth."

Molly put the letter which she had kept in her hand, onto the patio table.

"I will leave you to decide, I will respect whatever your decision is and hope you won't hate me!"

Molly went back indoors, she was shaking. She went upstairs to her bedroom and sat on her bed.

Emily sat and looked at the letter with her name on. She didn't need to make a big decision.

Molly cuddled the little pink teddy that she had kept for over 30 years.

Dinah's bear!

She turned and saw Emily standing in the doorway of her bedroom.

"Hello, Mum!" Emily ran over to Molly.

"It says that I was registered as Dinah May in Leeds registry office two days after my birth by Molly Jones, my mother.

Molly cried till she had no more tears left. She hugged her Dinah and it was hard to let her go.

They went back down the stairs and Emily made them both a sherry.

"There is something else you should know, Emily."

Molly told her about Jim, her father, and that he was also Jonathon's father.

"Have you told Jane?"

"She knows that Jonathon's father is also Dinah's father, but until we knew if you were my daughter she has said nothing to Jonathon. We can phone her now if you like. She knows that I was going to tell you tonight."

So the truth was out in the open now and Molly had not lost Emily. In fact, she had found her Dinah. Jonathon was astonished when Jane told him that James was also Emily's father and that they now knew for sure that Molly was her birth mother. Molly was so happy.

Emily had often wondered who her natural parents were, even though she had loved her adoptive parents.

She had not only found her mother, but also another brother.

Chapter 37

Margot's husband Peter had been busy contacting an agency that was able to trace adopted children. Letters received so far had not revealed any information as to where Sonny Jim had been taken after his adoption.

Peter had not told Margot that the news so far was negative. He just told her that these things take time.

Margot visited Norma and her family quite often and Norma and Barry had visited Peter and Margot for a weekend.

Norma's son was going to be married shortly so a lot of conversations between the two women were concerned with the clothes they were going to wear for the wedding.

A couple of months after Peter first contacted the agency a letter came which raised his hopes. The agency had traced the family to whom Sonny had been adopted only to find that the parents had both passed away.

A neighbour of the deceased parents told the investigator that the boy had moved to Maidstone in Kent, as far as she knew, after the death of his parents.

They now knew that the adopted name of the boy was David Nichols. So at least they had a name to go on.

A marriage had been registered for a David Nichols, with the correct date of birth several years ago, before he had moved to Kent.

So now the search was to be concentrated on the Kent area.

Peter still did not say anything to Margot as it still wasn't certain that this David Nichols was Sonny Jim.

The agency then told Peter that they were going to put an advert in the Kent Messenger asking for anyone by the name of David Nichols born in 1961 would contact the agency. They did warn Peter that often a lot of cranks answered these kinds of ads and also some who thought there was money at the end of it.

Two months went by and Peter had almost given up.

Then he got a letter from the agency. They had received a letter in reply to their advertisement that looked promising. They had received some replies that had turned out to be bogus when checked out, but they thought this one seemed genuine. They had enclosed a copy of the letter they had received in reply to the enquiries that the agency had sent to Mr Nichols.

Dear Sirs

I have answered your enquiries about my past as best I can.

My name is David Nichols and I was born on 16th August, 1961 in Leeds.

I have no knowledge of my natural parents as I was adopted by Frank and Peggy Nichols when I was about six or seven weeks old.

They have now sadly passed away. I moved to Kent after they died mainly to make a new start. I was married, but my wife became addicted to drink and has now also passed away.

I have never seen the original copy of my birth certificate. I asked my adoptive mother if she knew my real mother's name and all she knew was that it was something like Margaret and I was born in Leeds.

I understand from your letter that a family member would like to get in touch. As I now have no parents, this is something I would consider.

As Peter read this letter, his heart leapt. Could this lad be Margot's Sonny Jim?

He immediately replied to the letter and told them he wanted to come down Kent to see this Mr Nichols. He could not allow Margot to be disappointed if it all turned out wrong.

The agent said that they would check out all the details and possibly a DNA test could be done to ascertain if David was Margot's boy. Peter agreed and took hairs from Margot's hairbrush and even scooped up some nail clippings after she had been doing her nails. He was determined that he would be sure that David Nichols was Sonny Jim before he told Margot.

The particles of hair and nails were sent off and Peter waited impatiently for further news.

David had agreed to a DNA test also.

The agency told him when they expected the results of the DNA test.

Peter told Margot that he had to go to London on church business the week these results were due. Also the agency told him, David was coming to London for an interview with the agency, so Peter wanted to be in London for that interview.

He prayed so fervently that the news would be good but still said nothing to Margot.

The Agency had told Peter that he couldn't be present when they interviewed David because of privacy laws.

Margot was going shopping for wedding clothes with Norma in Leeds the day Peter went down to London. He expected to be there for a couple of days at least, but was determined to try and see this David.

He had booked into a Travel Lodge near to the Agency's office and settled down on the first evening. He intended to be at the Agency office fairly early the following morning.

The next day Peter arrived at the office just after ten o'clock. The receptionist obviously had been expecting Peter as she showed him into lounge area and offered him a cup of tea.

"I am Mr French's secretary he will be with you soon Reverend Sillers, I expect you are looking forward to finding out if the lad is your stepson!"

"Stepson? It hadn't occurred to Peter that he may soon have a stepson. The feeling gave him a warm glow!"

He sat and waited patiently.

Chapter 38

In Cheshire, Sharon was trying to put the hidden letter out of her mind. It kept niggling in her mind. She argued with herself,

"No I am not interested"

"Well what if…?"

"Shut up, not interested!"

And so it went on…

Rupert had gone to the Algarve with a group from the golf club for a week's golf. So Sharon had too much time to think. After three days she went up to her bedroom, lifted the mattress and took the crumpled letter out.

She sat on the bed and opened the letter.

The Red Lion
Enchester
Cheshire

Dear Sharon

I had hoped to speak to you directly, but this has seemed something that you did not want.

I have respected your wishes but now events have taken an unexpected turn.

You may wonder how I know you are the Sharon Peterson I was looking for, well you can blame your mother for that.

She came with a group of women to a charity ball, where I was helping with the catering. I saw her name on her badge and when I saw Peterson I just wondered if might be related to a Sharon.

I was serving the drinks and I got talking to her, a bit of flattery gets you everywhere with ladies of a certain age! .She got exceedingly drunk and I got her talking. I asked about her family, about grandchildren.

She told me of her daughter Sharon, who had got pregnant in the sixties but said her husband had taken care of it. "Sent her to Leeds and they sorted her out!"

So Sharon, or I suppose I should call you mother, I am your son, it seems.

The original birth certificate says you called me Dominic, well they changed that to Edward. They, my adoptive parents were all OK, until they found out I was gay, when I was 17, then they kicked me out.

I have lived here in Enchester ever since, working and living in the pub.

Why do I now want to see you now? I am not too well and not long for this world. I would have liked to have a hug from my mum before I meet my maker.

You did bring me into this world, for that I thank you, you know where I am. It will be good to see you.

Love

Dominic aka Edward

Sharon sat on her bed. Tears ran down her face, tears that she didn't know she could still shed. Inside she felt that longing that she had been covering up for many years.

She then got up, went to her wardrobe and found her coat and walking boots. It seemed she couldn't get her outdoor clothes on fast enough. She grabbed her car keys and got in the car and drove out of her driveway.

Oh shit, she thought, *I have no idea where Enchester is.*

She pulled into the first garage and bought a map book of Cheshire.

She was amazed, Enchester was only about ten miles from her home.

Only ten miles away all this time! she thought.

She kept seeing a picture of the beautiful child that she had given up in Leeds. She had tried so hard to eradicate the memory, but deep inside his little face was in her heart and as much as she fought it, he always would be...

All of a sudden, her father nor her husband meant anything, she needed to see her son.

It took her 20 minutes to find Enchester. It appeared to be a chocolate box little village. She parked outside the pub which displayed the 'Red Lion' sign. There was a church across the road, and it appeared that a lot of people were gathering outside the church doorway.

Sharon got out of her car and went up the old stone steps into the pub.

The bar was completely empty except for an old woman who was behind the bar.

"Hello, I am looking for Edward," she said hesitantly to the woman.

"And who might you be?"

Sharon thought for a minute and said, "Oh just a friend!"

The next words from the old woman nearly floored Sharon.

"You had better get over to the church if you want to say goodbye to the lad, they are burying him today. He passed away last Friday. God rest his soul." The old woman crossed herself as she said it.

Sharon felt her knees go from under her. The old woman brought a glass with a measure of brandy and sat her on a chair.

"Get this down you, then get yourself to the church!"

Sharon gulped the amber liquid down her throat and somehow walked to the church. She crept inside and sat on the nearest pew at the back of the church.

The coffin was covered by a large wreath of red flowers and a Manchester United shirt was draped under the flowers.

A man was standing by the coffin reading from a piece of paper.

"Edward will be much missed in the village. He was a lovely person. He would do anything for anyone as you all know.

When my mother and father adopted him, they had found a treasure, sadly they found it difficult to understand the way he wished to live his life. But he was my little brother and I loved him. He struggled with academia but when Old Sid over there put a spanner in his hands after he came to this village he was in his element and helped a lot of us out when our motors broke down.

When he found Nick his partner, he was so happy. But when Nick died last year, I think part of Eddy died too.

He did try to find his natural mother, but sadly wasn't able to. The world will be a sadder place without Edward."

His voice broke, and there wasn't a dry eye in the church.

Sharon thought her heart would break. She couldn't listen any more, she crept back out of the church while they were singing the final hymn.

She climbed back into her car and sobbed.

She watched as the coffin was reverently carried into the churchyard to the waiting grave. The lump in her throat and the pain in her chest were so bad.

The mourners left the churchyard and made their way to the pub.

Sharon just sat in her car, she couldn't think, she was afraid to allow her thoughts to manifest themselves.

A tap came on her car window. She looked up and the old woman from the pub stood there.

Sharon's first instinct was to drive off, but something in the old woman's eyes made her wind her window down.

"Come with me, love."

She had no idea why but she got out of the car and followed the old woman into the graveyard. She put two red roses into Sharon's hand but said nothing.

They walked slowly to the open grave. She waved the two men away who were obviously going to cover the coffin.

"Your son was a fine young man. The fact you are here now would please him."

"How did you know?" Sharon said quietly.

"You have the same eyes as Edward, and only a mother would weep as you did. I know because in the next grave is my son Nick, Edward's partner."

Sharon gently let one of the roses fall onto her Dominic's coffin, the other she took and placed on Nick's grave.

"Son, I am so sorry, I loved you so much, but I put myself first, please forgive me."

The old woman took her arm and led her back to her car.

"Don't look back, he had a happy life in the village. He used to come and clean my hens out for me, and he got to know my son then.

Nick went to London for a few years but wanted to come back home.

Edward and Nick became close after he returned from London. We didn't find out that Nick had contracted the disease for some time

Edward nursed my Nick for two years until he passed away.

He was diagnosed with the Aids himself after we lost Nick.

I will look after both their graves, now get yourself home."

"I never forgot my child, but my family …"

"Hush you don't need to explain, it was a different time back then. Go back to your life, he is at rest now."

Sharon started the car and with a heavy heart drove back home.

Chapter 39

Peter had returned from his trip in London with no further news. David Nichols had at the last minute cancelled his trip to London. Peter felt very cross, but there was nothing he could do. The DNA results had also not come back. Apparently there was a backlog of tests and they would just have to be patient.

He had arranged with his postman to deliver all his mail to his office at the church and given express instructions to the Agency to be sure and address any letters direct to the church.

After two weeks Peter was thinking of phoning the agency, but then kept putting it off as he was afraid that the DNA would be negative, at least in not knowing he felt there was still hope.

Every night, before he locked up the church he said a little prayer, as he knew how much all this meant to his beloved Margot.

Margot noticed that Peter seemed a little out of sorts and she asked him if there was anything worrying him.

"No, my love, just a few parishioner problems. Old Mrs Graves is really poorly but wants to stay in her own home, even though the doctor wants to hospitalize her."

Margot took Peter's hand.

"I will go along tomorrow for a visit in the morning. I understand how she feels. She was born in that house and so was her mother. She just wants to die there."

Peter knew that Mrs Graves loved Margot as did all his parishioners and she would love to see Margot in the morning.

Margot picked some flowers from her garden the next morning and hurried off to see the old lady Peter walked with her till they reached the church, gave her a hug and Margot carried onto Mrs Graves cottage.

Peter saw Sam, the postman leaning his bike against the church wall.

"Morning, Sam, how's that new baby of yours?"

"Morning, vicar. He's bonny, the missus is convinced he is saying Dadda.

Here's your mail, quite a lot today. I see the Mothers Union have got a lot of post. They have started this patchwork class and they keep sending off for new patterns. My old Ma is really getting into it. Keeps cutting up my old shirts, I'm afraid to put anything down in case she gets the scissors on em!"

Peter laughed, as the classes were one of Margot's ideas and he had the same problem.

He waited till Sam had cycled off down the road before he scanned through the post. He found a letter postmarked London. He had felt so guilty at lying to Margot about his trip to London and thought that he had better tell her the truth. He knew they could face whatever the outcome together so he decided that he would tell her what he had done and then they could open the letter that evening. He put the letter in his jacket pocket.

He went into his church and knelt down and once again asked if God would help Margot whatever the news. As he got up, Margot came into the church.

"Darling, Mrs Graves is very weak and has asked me to come and find you."

They went back to the little cottage together. Nellie Graves was in a bed in the parlour. She hadn't been able to climb the stairs for some time.

When she saw Peter, she lifted her hand and smiled.

162

"Thank you for coming, vicar, I am ready to meet my maker, will you say a few words?"

Margot took the old lady's hand and Peter took the other. As he was halfway through the Lord's Prayer, the old lady closed her eyes and breathed her last breath.

Margot leaned forward and kissed her cheek.

The doctor was called and the district nurse to attend to the formalities. The undertakers came and took her body to the chapel of rest.

Peter phoned her one surviving relative, a distant cousin in the next village.

Peter and Margot walked slowly home, feeling sad but relieved that the old lady was at last at peace.

Nellie had been a character and knew that there would be a good turnout at her funeral and she would be missed.

"I will make us a nice cup of tea before you go back to the church; I have made your favourite cherry cake"

Margot put the kettle on and cut a generous slice of her newly baked cake.

"Don't forget you have the Wilson's coming at 3:30 to discuss their son's christening."

Peter drank his tea and enjoyed his over large piece of cake, then walked back to the church for his meeting with the Wilsons.

After the christening meeting, he made himself a cup of tea, he knew he wouldn't have time to go back home before his next appointment.

The head mistress of the local primary school had asked him to give a talk to the children about the dangers of talking to strangers. She had felt the children would be less intimidated by Peter than by the local constable, who was not very child friendly and talked very loudly. There had been reports of attempted child abductions in a nearby town, so Mrs Carberry the head mistress was taking all the precautions she felt necessary to protect her charges.

Peter knew most of the children and their families and he knew Margot was very popular in the Sunday school that a lot

163

of them came to. After his talk the children showed him some of their artwork, which he praised greatly, which pleased the children.

The parents had come into school after lessons to listen to Peters talk and by the time they had all left. He was feeling more than a little tired.

When Peter got home, Margot had just lifted a wonderful smelling casserole out of the oven.

"Come and sit down, darling, it's been a busy day today."

Margot served Peter up with a bowl of stew, followed by a homemade apple crumble and custard. After he had eaten he went with his newspaper to his favourite chair and Margot noticed he soon dropped off to sleep.

Margot knew that his nap would not last long. He seemed to be able to have these power naps and wake refreshed soon after.

Margot washed the dishes then sat opposite her snoozing husband with her knitting.

True to form Peter opened his eyes half an hour later feeling refreshed.

Margot had switched the TV on, but she wasn't really watching the political debate that was taking place.

"Can I switch this off? There is something I must talk to you about," Peter said.

"Yes we must discuss Nellie's funeral service darling, it doesn't look as though her cousin is very interested in doing it, and everyone loved Nellie!"

"No, love this is about us. We have always been honest with each other, now there is something I need to tell you!"

Margot put down her knitting,

"You are not ill are you, please don't tell me that!"

"No, no I am fine. Please don't be cross with me as I didn't tell you the truth but my intentions were to protect you from worrying.

"When I went down to London a few weeks ago, it was not on church business. I had been in contact with an agency who are legally allowed to access adoption records. They wrote to me to tell me that they may have some information. I didn't want to tell you in case it was another dead end. They have had some of those and it would get my hopes up only to be dashed when they turned out not to be your boy. You didn't deserve to go through that.

"They found that a baby born on Sonny's date of birth in Leeds.

"He had been adopted by a family called Nichols and they called the baby David. So they now had a name to look for. Several David Nichols were found but one in particular appeared a possible match."

Margot held her breath.

"I took some hairs from your hairbrush and some nail clippings and sent them to the agency, which then sent them to be tested along with some samples from this David Nichols. This would show if there was a match and if this young man was Sonny.

"When I went to London, I was disappointed and cross, as this young man cancelled his appointment to be interviewed by the agency. There was also news from the laboratories that they had a long backlog of tests and couldn't say when they would have the results. So I came back with no news and I have felt guilty ever since for doing it behind your back."

Margot went over and took Peter's hand.

"You have tried, I understand, love. I have waited 30 years so a little longer won't matter and it may all come to nothing."

"But, my love, a letter came this morning, which I haven't opened. As I felt, this is one letter we should open together. If it is bad news then we will continue looking."

Peter extracted the letter and gave it to Margot.

She carefully opened the letter and quietly read the contents.

She looked at Peter, her eyes said it all. Peter knew what the letter told them.

Chapter 40

Sharon drove home slowly. Her whole body felt numb. Her brain kept screaming like a raging banshee! The voices in her head blocked everything out. She walked round her garden, the birds all stopped singing. The flowers looked sad and limp, nothing was right. Her eyes couldn't focus, she couldn't cry, she couldn't speak and she didn't want to think.

She unlocked the house and went up to her bedroom. She went to writing bureau and sat down and wrote two letters.

One letter she put a stamp on and took it downstairs and put it on the hall table for her daily help to post, on the other letter she just wrote 'Rupert' on the envelope and leant it up against her mirror on her dressing table.

The following morning Rupert returned having taken an early flight from Portugal. He was surprised to find the front door unlocked. He dropped his golf clubs into his downstairs office and called out to Sharon.

On receiving no reply, he went up to their bedroom to take his jacket off.

Sharon lay on the bed, "Hi, Darling, having a snooze?"

He bent over and was going to kiss her when he saw her face. He touched her cheek, it was ice cold and bluish.

"My God, what have you done?" He saw the empty sleeping tablet bottle and the half-empty vodka bottle.

Rupert went to the phone in a daze, His princess was dead!

After the doctor had been, the local police came to the house.

The letter was found on the dressing table, as Rupert read it the tears ran down his face.

Dear Rupert
I cannot stay here. I have been living a lie. Thank you for loving me, but I was not the person you thought I was, not your princess.
Please don't blame yourself, it's better I go.
Love
S xx

The daily help had come to work as usual but had been sent home. She picked up the other letter and posted it on her way back home.

The second letter came through Molly's letterbox the next day.

Sharon had always portrayed herself as a self-confident lady in the odd letter she had sent to Molly over the years. No regrets over the decision she had made years ago in Leeds. Molly was never fully convinced that this was actually what Sharon felt.

When Molly read the letter, she knew she had been right.

The letter brought tears to Molly's eyes. She knew it would be too late for any earthly help.

"Poor Sharon, she thought she could try to forget, but it never goes away."

Molly phoned Jane, she was almost too choked to speak.

"It's so awful, Jane, it's Sharon…" That is all she could get out.

Jane heard the anguish in Molly's voice.

"I will come straight over, is Emily there with you?"

"No, don't want to worry her, yes please come over."

Molly put the phone down and reread the letter again.

My Dear Friend Molly,
Please understand what I do is the only thing left for me. I abandoned my baby because I wanted to enjoy my life.

He needed me I turned my back on him because I was too selfish, selfish, selfish!

He was willing to forgive me, he came to find me, I turned my back, now I can't forgive myself.

When I look in the mirror, I see an ugly selfish bitch!

Today I saw my boy, my baby, buried. I couldn't even stand at his grave with his friends and weep I was too ashamed.

Ashamed of myself. He was dying and wanted me, I turned my back.

Molly I think you knew I needed him, but I wouldn't listen.

Annie said years ago we were on the road to ruin, she was right for me.

I hope you can forgive me.

My boy is buried in Enchester churchyard, if you are ever near would you perhaps lay some flowers for my Dominic.

I deserve nothing, but my boy deserves to be remembered with love.

Thank you and the others (you know who I mean) for being my friends.

Sharon.

Molly poured herself a drink, then heard her front door open.

Emily ran in, Jane had phoned her.

By the time Jane got there, Molly felt a little calmer. When Jane read the letter, they all wept again.

"Do you suppose it is too late, perhaps we should ring?"

At that moment, Molly's phone rang. Molly picked up the receiver.

A man's voice asked if it was Molly he was speaking to.

"This is Rupert Fleming, I found your number in my wife's address book. Our cleaner says that she posted a letter to you yesterday.

Did you receive a letter? You see my wife took her own life last night."

Rupert's voice broke and he was obviously crying.

"I wondered what was in the letter. I have no idea why she has done this; I thought she may have said something in her letter to you."

Molly had put the phone on speaker so that Jane could hear the conversation. Jane looked at Molly and shook her head.

"Yes I got a letter, but there was nothing unusual in her letter. I am so sad to hear your news; please can you let us know when the funeral is. Sharon was a lovely lady, I am so upset for you. What a terrible shock!"

Rupert mumbled his thanks and just before he hung up he said,

"Would it be possible to see the letter Sharon sent you?"

"Oh Rupert, I wrote a reply to Sharon this morning straight after I received her letter, it's here waiting for me to post. I always shred my letters once I write the reply, so I am sorry it's in the bin."

Rupert said goodbye and hung up. It was obvious that he was devastated at the loss of his wife.

"I couldn't be the one to tell Sharon's secret," Molly sadly said.

"That's why I shook my head, she hasn't told her husband about Dominic obviously."

The two women felt so sad. Emily also even though she hadn't known Sharon or Dominic.

"We will let the other girls know. Perhaps they will come to her funeral."

Chapter 41

Margot passed the letter to Peter.

Tears were streaming down her face.

"You found Sonny Jim." That was all she could say. The love she felt for her husband was over whelming her.

Peter read the letter. It appeared that the DNA test showed conclusively that David Nichols was Margot's son. It also said that Mr Nichols was looking forward to making contact, but until the agency received written permission from Peter and Margot, they could not release any addresses to Mr Nichols.

Margot started to worry that she would have to wash all the curtains and have a spring clean before she met her son.

"I will have to get the spare room redecorated as I hope he will come and stay."

So many thoughts ran through Margot's mind, she was in a state of euphoric panic. She couldn't help smiling, sleep strangely enough came easily that night. When Peter got up, Margot was shampooing the lounge carpets and the lounge curtains were in the washing machine.

Margot was singing as she worked. Peter smiled to himself; to see Margot so happy was a tonic.

Peter went to the church leaving Margot in a fury of cleaning, dusting and hoovering. By teatime, the house smelt of baking, the house shone and Margot was feeling happily exhausted.

"I had better go up and have a bath, I look like a washer woman," Margot took off her pinafore and took the pins out of her hair.

As she was about to go up to the bathroom, the front door bell rang.

"Probably the paper boy with the evening paper, I will wait and take it up with me to read while I soak in the bath," Margot said giving her hair a brush.

She heard a conversation going on in the front hall of the vicarage.

Peter came back into the room, "We have a visitor, darling," he stepped to one side and a blond-haired man walked into the room.

"Hello, Mum!"

Margot couldn't stand, "Sonny Jim, oh my darling boy."

David smiled at his mother, he had been told of the name that he had been given. He put his arms round the shaking woman who he knew for sure was the mother that had loved him and waited for him for over 30 years.

"I haven't come on my own, Mum,"

Peter had gone back out into the hall and came back in with a small boy holding one hand and a little girl holding the other.

"This is Mark and Mandy, your grandson and granddaughter."

Margot was speechless.

David told them that he had waited till Mr French at the Agency had left his office to get him a cup of tea and he had picked up some of the paperwork from his desk and found Margot and Peter's address.

Once he had known that Margot was definitely his mother, he just couldn't wait to come and find her.

The reason he had cancelled his first appointment was because Mandy had a high temperature and he couldn't leave her.

It was obvious that David struggled to juggle childcare with his work, but the children came first.

Margot had found her son and much more.

The first visit lasted three days. Every opportunity David found he would load his old car up and head up to see Margot and Peter.

With each visit Margot and Peter learnt more of David's life.

The children's mother had sunk into alcoholism and David had taken the children and moved to Kent. A year later he had been told that she was dead. The children didn't even remember their mother.

He worked as a postman and he had become friendly with another postman whose wife offered to look after David's two children along with her own. She took the children to school with her own and picked them up after school. David came and took the home for their tea, so it worked very well. Extra money for his friend's wife and his children were being looked after well.

When the children's summer holidays came, Margot had asked David if the children could stay for the whole holidays. He was happy and the children were delighted.

When David brought them up, Peter asked tentatively, "I suppose you could be a postman anywhere. What about coming to live a bit nearer?"

David looked at Margot who sat playing 'Happy Families' with Mandy, who was laughing at something Margot had said.

"If I could find a job up here and somewhere to live I would move tomorrow, Peter. The kids love you and Mum and we would all love to be able to see more of you both."

"We have this huge house and Margot would be so happy to have you all here with us. But the decision is yours, son." The word son just slipped out.

"Can I call you Dad, it seems right somehow. I have been trying to pluck up courage to ask for a while."

Peter was choked, he just hugged Sonny Jim.

Both he and Margot still called him Sonny and he liked it.

So Peter went back down to Kent with Sonny, hired a truck and between them they moved Margot's family into the vicarage.

Margot was the happiest Grandma in the world she told everyone.

Her only sadness was the death of Sharon.

Chapter 42

Molly had written to Norma, Margot and Annie with the sad news about Sharon. They had all phoned and said they would like to go to Cheshire for the funeral.

Molly and Jane were going to drive down and Jonathon offered to do the driving and he suggested hiring a Minibus. So Margot and Norma travelled down by train to Molly's and they went down to Cheshire together in the minibus.

A hotel was booked near to the Crematorium where the funeral was to take place. Emily had asked if anyone would mind if she came with them, as she felt she knew Sharon from all the stories she had been told.

Annie was coming up from the south by train and Jonathon was going to collect her from the nearest station and bring her to the hotel.

They found their hotel and settled themselves into their rooms. Molly shared with Emily and Jane in a family room. Jonathon had a single and the other three women shared another three-bed family room.

After they had freshened up they met in the dining room for their evening meal.

Rupert had invited them to the house the following morning for a light lunch before the funeral, at two o'clock. Their conversation was regarding what they should say to Rupert and Sharon's family. They all agreed that no mention could be made about Dominic, as it was obvious that Rupert still didn't know anything about Sharon's son. It was going to be an awkward meeting.

After they had eaten the girls changed into their pyjamas and met in Molly's room.

"This takes me back," Molly said laughing. "But at least no-one is coming to take our children away this time."

Molly had brought up a bottle of wine from the bar, "I think we should drink a little toast to the memory of Sharon and Dominic, God rest their souls."

The girls raised their glasses in a silent salute.

Emily and Jonathon had stayed downstairs to have a final nightcap.

They had become very close as brother and sister over the months since the revelations of their births. Emily loved Jonathon and Laura's children and they loved her.

"Well I'm going up; the oldies were going to have some kind of pyjama party I think in Molly's room, bless their cotton socks!"

They both chuckled as they went up to their respective rooms.

The following morning they all had breakfast together, then retired to their rooms to dress for the funeral.

Sharon was a colourful character so they had decided not to wear black.

Jonathon had enquired at the hotel how to get to Rupert's home so they wouldn't get lost.

They were all astounded at the large houses and plush gardens they passed on the way. It was obvious that it was a very rich area.

"Eh look in that garden there is a big fountain and naked statues!"

Margot said, "Look, that one has a swimming pool." Emily was amazed.

When they arrived at Rupert's house, it was another large house.

Large metal gates swung open as they pulled up and a gardener was sweeping leaves from the velvet lawns.

A tall, distinguished-looking grey haired man came out onto the patio to greet them.

"That must be Rupert, what a distinguished man!" Molly said.

They introduced themselves one by one.

"Thank you for coming. Please come in." They had guessed that Rupert had asked them to the house as he needed answers to questions about Sharon's past.

After they had drunk the toast the evening before to Sharon, in Molly's bedroom, the girls had discussed what they were going to say, or not say to Rupert.

It would be very awkward and they had no intention of upsetting any of Sharon's family or disclosing her secret.

Molly had been delegated to ward off any awkward conversations. She was quick thinking and hopefully she could divert any probing questions.

"How did you all meet? I know Sharon used to write to you occasionally and kept in touch."

"We met over 30 years ago, Rupert, just a group of girls doing what girls do. We are so sad for your loss. Are Sharon's parents still alive, it must be very sad for her family?"

They had decided that a good way to ward off any probing was to reply with questions of their own.

"Sharon's mother passed away two years ago and her father has had a stroke, so doesn't really comprehend what has happened. Now please help yourselves to some lunch and tea and coffee, there is wine if you prefer."

They entered the beautiful lounge where a table was laid with sandwiches, quiches and salads. None of them were really hungry, but took a sandwich each and a waitress brought teas and coffees.

Rupert went off to speak to other guests who were dressed in black, but soon came back to their group. He pulled up a chair and with tears in his eyes he sat down next to Molly.

"I am sorry to seem as though I am interrogating you, Molly, but I feel there is part of my Sharon's life that I know nothing about. She sometimes looked far away and in the night she would talk in her sleep. I asked her father some years ago, and he snapped my head off as if I was suggesting some black past. Does the name Dominic mean anything to any of you?"

Emily and Jonathon moved away, the tension was almost tangible.

Molly looked at Jane. Margot wanted to cry, Annie looked at her feet, knowing her face would give something away.

Jane stood up and said, "Shall we take a walk in your beautiful garden, Rupert? She looked at Margot, Norma and Annie, they all nodded, they knew this man deserved to know the truth. They couldn't lie to this man who was so devastated at losing the woman he had obviously loved.

Molly and Jane walked out into the garden with Rupert. What they were about to tell him they hoped would in some way help him to understand that he was not at fault for this tragedy.

The sins of the fathers are often visited on the children. If Sharon's father had not been so intransigent, maybe the outcome would have been different.

Jane and Molly gently told Sharon's husband about Dominic. How scared Sharon was that her family would disown her, and on the other hand she wanted to keep her child. It was a cleft stick.

When Molly explained about the last day of her life, finding Dominic too late and how she felt she had let the boy down. The despair in her last letter was something Molly couldn't tell Rupert. The letter which Molly had destroyed. It would have been too cruel to let Rupert read the depths of his wife's heart break.

Rupert wanted a moment on his own, so the girls left him to gather himself ready for the coming funeral.

When the cortege arrived at the house, Rupert's friends gathered round and they all drove to the crematorium.

There was quite a crowd already gathered at the little chapel. The group from Rupert's golf club with their designer wives. The neighbours pulling up in there prestigious vehicles.

177

The villagers standing in a group away from the main mourners. One old woman caught Molly's eye. She was standing apart from the rest of the crowd, almost as if she didn't want to be seen. Her eyes were reddened as though she had been weeping.

After the ceremony the main party returned to Rupert's house, but Molly and the others wanted to go over to Enchester to find Dominic's grave. They found the little village and went into the pub preferring to sit quietly in their own little group to remember their friend, before they went to the graveyard.

They were chatting about Sharon's colourful language the day she had gone into labour, there were a few things that made them laugh, not a lot sadly.

As they sat around the table, Molly noticed the old woman who had been at the crematorium come into the pub. She took her coat off and went behind the bar and started serving.

Molly was curious. She said she would get more drinks. They were only on soft drinks and Margot and Annie were drinking tea.

"Could we have another pot of tea for two, please, two Coca Colas and two orange juices and one fizzy water?" she asked the old woman.

The woman got the cold drinks, "I will bring the tea over to you, dear."

Molly went back with the tray of drinks. Shortly after, the tray with the teapot was delivered.

Molly spoke softly to the old woman.

"You were at our friend Sharon's funeral. Was she a friend?"

The old lady looked so sad.

"Yes I saw you and your friends."

"We were wondering if you know where Dominic is buried," Molly asked her.

"When you have finished your drinks, I will show you."

Molly and the others left the table a little later and followed the woman.

She took them into the churchyard. At the newly covered grave, she stopped.

"We knew him as Edward, but his gravestone will have the name his mother gave him as well.

"The grave next to this is his partner, Nick…my son.

"This is where I last saw your friend. She couldn't live with the boy, but once she found him she couldn't live without him!"

A tear ran down the old lady's face, she then walked slowly back to the pub. Molly asked Jonathon to go back to the mini bus. She had asked Rupert if she could have some flowers from Sharon's garden which he had been pleased to give. Jonathon brought them and gave them to Molly, who laid them gently onto the new grave.

They all stood in silence, thinking their own thoughts. Remembering the past, but knowing at least they all had a future.

Jonathon put his arm around his mother and Emily took Molly's hand.

"I guess we are the lucky ones, you have all been down a long hard road, emotionally and physically, but we survived.

"Some were not so lucky.

"Rest in peace Sharon, Dominic and Nick, we hope you will all be together in a kinder world."

There was no conversation on the way back to the hotel. They packed their bags and Jonathon drove Annie back to the station and then turned northwards to home; Norma to her son, Billy, and Margot to her Sonny Jim.

The following spring, Molly received a letter from Rupert. He had decided that Sharon would like her ashes buried with her son. He enclosed a colour photograph of the stone he had erected next to Dominic's grave.

The stone read,

SHARON FLEMING
1944- 1992
Beloved wife of Rupert
Mother to Dominic.

Death is only a shadow
On the pathway to Heaven
May you find there what you
Couldn't find on earth.
R.I.P.

Molly sent a copy of the photo to all the girls. Annie looked at the picture and saw the cherry blossom that had blown across the graveyard from an overhanging tree. It reminded her of another day a long time ago.